'Hold it right th....,' interrupted. 'You don't have to explain yourself to me about anything.

'You're a free spirit and want to remain so, and I don't blame you. We've been crowding you and I'm sorry.'

'It isn't like that at all,' she protested. 'You have nothing to be sorry about, Marc. It's just that I hope to go back to Paris one day, and I wouldn't want the children to get too attached to me and be upset when I leave.'

'So we haven't charmed you enough to make you want to stay?'

'It isn't a case of that, and if I do go back it won't be until I'm sure that my father will be all right without me. You do understand, don't you?' she pleaded. 'It's just that I've lived there all my life, the same as you have lived here all your life, and I'm sure that you wouldn't want to leave this place to go and live in Paris?'

He was tempted to tell her he'd go to the North Pole if she asked him to, but Giselle was young and very beautiful, and he was a widower with two children that he loved too much to think of uprooting. That was a decision he wasn't going to have to make, as she'd just made it clear that she was merely passing through the village and passing through his life.

Abigail Gordon loves to write about the fascinating combination of medicine and romance from her home in a Cheshire village. She is active in local affairs and is even called upon to write the script for the annual village pantomime! Her eldest son is a hospital manager and helps with all her medical research. As part of a close-knit family, she treasures having two of her sons living close by and the third one not too far away. This also gives her the added pleasure of being able to watch her delightful grandchildren growing up.

Recent titles by the same author:

COMING BACK FOR HIS BRIDE
A SURGEON'S MARRIAGE WISH
HER SURGEON BOSS

A
FRENCH DOCTOR
AT ABBEYFIELDS

BY
ABIGAIL GORDON

MILLS & BOON®

First published in Great Britain 2006
Large Print edition 2006
Harlequin Mills & Boon Limited,
Eton House, 18-24 Paradise Road,
Richmond, Surrey TW9 1SR

© Abigail Gordon 2006

ISBN-13: 978 0 263 19524 8
ISBN-10:   0 263 19524 4

Set in Times Roman 17¼ on 20½ pt.
17-0906-49959

Printed and bound in Great Britain
by Antony Rowe Ltd, Chippenham, Wiltshire

CHAPTER ONE

THE auction was being held in the old livery stables at the far end of the village and as she looked around her Giselle imagined she could smell the horses that had been tethered beneath its wooden slatted ceiling in years gone by.

The feeling of unreality that she'd had ever since boarding the aircraft in Paris, *en route* for Manchester Airport, was still strong within her as she looked around at the assortment of would-be purchasers gathered there.

What was she doing in this quiet English backwater? she kept asking herself, and always came the same answer. Her father, who had lived in Paris for the last twenty-five years with her French mother, had dismayed her by announcing that he wanted to go back to his roots, to the village where he had lived as a boy.

The fact that he had those sort of yearnings had been shattering enough, but two things had made it even more incredible. Firstly, he had told her what he had in mind on the very day that they'd buried her mother in a French cemetery, and secondly, he had announced that he'd heard from an old friend still living in the village that the house where he'd lived in his youth was up for sale by auction.

She had listened to him, aghast.

'How can you be thinking such thoughts?' she'd exclaimed. 'We have only just buried *maman*.'

'Exactly,' he'd said sadly. 'And I can't bear the thought of Paris without her. We came here when you were two years old because Celeste was so homesick for her beautiful city. The firm of accountants where I was a director had a French office and I transferred, but now she is gone, Giselle. The cancer took her from us and I want to go home.'

He had looked tired and older than his seventy-two years, and she'd said anxiously, '*You* can't go to England to bid for your old home, *papa*. We have both cared for *maman* over many weeks and you're exhausted. I don't want to lose you, too.'

'Then *you* will have to do it,' he'd said, and she'd thought dismally that she didn't want to leave Paris to live in a country where it was always raining, and in the countryside, of all places. Yet she couldn't leave her father to fend for himself after losing her mother. In the months to come he would need her there beside him.

But *she* was happiest in the throb of city life. Smart restaurants, theatres and designer shops. When she had free time from her job as a registrar in a hospital in the city, she enjoyed them to the full.

Also, Raoul was in Paris, lean, dark, and attentive. Though she hadn't seen much of him while her mother had been ill. He didn't like anything to do with sickness and questioned frequently why she couldn't find a job that was more chic.

She'd taken extended leave from the hospital to nurse her mother and by now would have been back on the wards and getting her life together again if her father hadn't faced her with such a bombshell.

But instead here she was, amongst strangers in a Cheshire village, miles away from home, about to start bidding in a property auction for a house called Abbeyfields.

Her father had been in touch with the agents before she'd left France and when he'd told her what the reserve on the property was, Giselle had been horrified.

'Can we afford that?' she'd gasped.

'Yes, if we have to,' he'd said, undismayed, and she'd realised then just how determined he was to go back to where he had come from.

James Morrison, the friend who had told him that the house was for sale, owned a small garden centre in the village, and Giselle had stayed with him and his wife the night before, after the agent had shown her around the property that she'd come to bid for.

He had been most effusive as they'd toured the old limestone-built house that her father wanted to come back to, noting the elegance of the prospective buyer and at the same registering a lack of enthusiasm that he wouldn't have expected from anyone viewing one of the most attractive detached houses in the area. But, then, she was from Paris of all places, so a quiet hamlet like this wasn't going to knock her sideways.

Giselle had gone back to the office with him to discuss some of the details on the brochure, and as she was leaving she had almost collided with a man in a hurry.

He had been broad-shouldered, dressed in casual tweeds, with a fresh complexion, a neatly trimmed head of thick fair hair, and deep blue eyes that had twinkled across at her as he'd said, 'Sorry, my fault.'

She'd acknowledged the apology with a nod of the head and had gone on her way, too apprehensive about what the morrow would bring to give him another thought. Supposing someone outbid her, she kept thinking. The agent had said there'd been a lot of interest. The last thing she wanted was to go back to France with the news that someone else had bought Abbeyfields.

As she looked around the auction room Giselle saw the man from the day before seated across from her. He was reading the list of properties to be auctioned, but as if sensing that he was being observed he looked up and met her glance and this time he wasn't smiling. He just nodded briefly and went back to what he'd been doing.

Giselle wasn't to know it but Marc Bannerman had been visiting the estate agent's for the same reason as herself. He intended bidding for Abbeyfields.

It stood in a quiet cul-de-sac just off the main street with views of the surrounding peaks from the upper windows. He had decided that it would make a perfect surgery with living accomodation, instead of the present one that was no longer big enough to cope with the increasing number of those who were moving to the countryside.

When the estate agent had told him that the smartly dressed woman with the glossy brown hair and piquant face was also interested in the property he had thought dryly that here was another townie with ideas of moving into the village.

He didn't normally have any quarrel with that. They had as much right to live there as he had. It was a beautiful place, with its limestone cottages, old established shops and the peaks, always the peaks, towering above it. Away from the noise and bustle of the nearest town, it was a haven of peace. The perfect place for Tom and Alice to grow up in, especially if he was successful in buying Abbeyfields.

Giselle would have liked the house to have been one of the first properties to be auctioned, so that the ordeal would soon be over, but it was way back in the catalogue and as she listened to the proceedings she could feel her heartbeat quickening and her stomach beginning to churn.

So much hung on this, she thought. Her father wanted the house called Abbeyfields so much and he deserved a little happiness after all those months of watching her mother die. Suddenly her apprehension became determination. He was going to have it. If she had to offer every penny they possessed, he was going to have it.

So far the man seated across from her hadn't bid on anything and she wondered which property he was interested in. She was soon to find out.

When the bidding for Abbeyfields began he took no part in it and for some reason that she didn't understand Giselle was relieved. The cool glance he'd bestowed upon her before the proceedings had begun had increased her nervousness. She'd known instinctively that he belonged to this place and recognised *her* for the outsider that she was.

But as the not so keen and those who were not prepared to go over a certain price began to drop out of the bidding, he began to make his voice heard and soon it was just the two of them.

Panic was rising inside her. He was so calm and composed, she thought. Just as determined as she was to buy the house that had been her father's boyhood home. The deep blue eyes that had been twinkly the day before were like an arctic sea and she wished she could run away and hide.

Then incredibly it was over. After her last bid there was no follow-up offer from her opponent. The auctioneer was making his last call and into the silence that followed he banged his gavel and the house was theirs, hers and her father's.

In that moment she was already saying goodbye to Paris, but hopefully not to Raoul. Although would he want to have to keep crossing the Channel to be with her in an English country backwater?

As she was leaving the auction rooms the man who had been bidding against her appeared at her side. 'Congratulations,' he said. 'I hope that you'll be very happy living in Abbeyfields.' As she dredged up a smile Giselle thought that he didn't mean it and was probably wishing her miles away…and if he was, it was no different than what she was wishing herself.

So much for that, Marc Bannerman was thinking sombrely as he strode off towards the village practice that he ran with the help of a junior doctor and his elderly father-in-law.

He'd known there was a lot of interest in the house and had been prepared to bid high, but the woman who had outbid him, a stranger who had appeared out of the blue, had been prepared to go higher, and with two children to support he'd had to draw back.

Morning surgery had just finished and Stanley Pollard, his father-in-law, and Craig Richards, the trainee GP, were eagerly waiting to hear if the practice was being moved to Abbeyfields.

He shook his head.

'I'm afraid not,' he said. 'I was outbid by a stranger. A brunette with beautiful violet eyes and a large bank balance.'

'I'll wager that would be the young woman who stayed at the garden centre with the Morrisons last night,' his father-in-law said. 'James was in for a check-up this morning and he said that she'd flown over from France to attend the auction.'

'From France?' Marc nodded thoughtfully. 'I could tell she didn't come from around these parts. Did he say what she was called and why she was staying with them?'

'It seems that the Morrisons know her father and James said her name was Giselle something or other.'

'Sounds interesting,' young Craig said with a grin. 'How long is she staying with them?'

'She was intending to leave the moment the auction was over,' the elderly GP told him, and Marc thought that today's setback wasn't going to be just his disappointment. The children would be upset, too.

The house had a few green acres with it. Its name came from an old abbey that used to stand in those same fields. Alice and Tom had been looking forward to playing there, instead of being confined to the small garden of the semi-detached that he and Amanda had bought when they'd married.

But it was no use crying over spilt milk, he told himself as he prepared to do the greater share of the home visits that had been asked for. Abbeyfields had been sold, and not to him. So it was going to be a case of looking elsewhere.

He didn't know why he'd congratulated the woman who'd bought it, considering that he didn't know her from Adam. It had been curiosity, he supposed, but it hadn't got him anywhere. She'd just given him a sickly smile and hurried out of the auction rooms without any show of pleasure.

He hoped that she wasn't one of the wealthy who were buying properties in the area to rent out. It would be the last straw if the house had been bought by someone who wasn't going to live in it.

He'd sensed a sort of nervous determination in her while they'd been bidding against each other and she hadn't faltered, which had told him that she wanted Abbeyfields just as much as he did. It would be interesting to see what happened next. Would she do it up, modernise it, or leave it in its original state. He hoped that it would be the latter. The house had only had two previous owners and they'd both treated it with respect.

On the return flight Giselle was facing up to the future. She kept telling herself that Paris wasn't the other side of the world. Frequent flights and the Channel Tunnel would make it easy to get there if she was desperate to see the city…and Raoul. His reaction to her news would be a good guideline by which to judge his true feelings for her.

If she had any doubts about his reaction, she had none about her father's. She'd phoned him from the airport and he'd been delighted to hear that Abbeyfields was now theirs. Giselle wished she could share his joy.

Apart from her original reluctance to move to the English countryside, she now had a feeling of guilt. The man who'd fought her for the house in the confines of some old livery stables had been a charitable loser. He had come across and congratulated her, but she hadn't been able to find a word to say to him because *she* didn't want the house. She'd been feeling bad inside because she'd taken it from him.

Had his need to buy it been greater than hers? she wondered. Possibly, but it couldn't have been greater than her father's. She was going to have to console herself with that thought.

Raoul, who owned a boutique in one of the smart shopping areas in Paris, was not at all pleased to hear that she was moving to England. He made it clear that the only arrangement he would countenance would be for her to live in London, as he sometimes went over for fashion shows and suchlike. She was told that he was not prepared to travel to the 'wilds of Cheshire' to be with her, so she had better change her mind.

'I can't do that,' she'd told him flatly. 'Not at the present time. My father needs me now that we have lost *maman*. Maybe I will be able to come back in a few months when he has settled in and had time to recover from her death. In the meantime, I will have to find employment once I'm there, and as I don't want to be away from him for hours on end it won't be easy.'

A customer had been hovering and Raoul said casually, 'So keep in touch. If I come to London, I'll give you a ring.'

Giselle left the shop thinking she'd been a fool to think he cared. The kind of ring he'd just mentioned was the only sort that would ever be forthcoming from Raoul.

They'd sold the apartment in Paris. The furniture had been shipped over by container, and as they drove up to Abbeyfields in the taxi they'd picked up at the airport, the expression on her father's face made up for everything that Giselle had misgivings about.

'Didn't you ever want to come back before?' she asked gently.

'Yes, many a time, but your mother would have been worried if she'd thought that she wasn't the only one to yearn for home.'

'I love you,' she told him chokily, and vowed that never by word or deed would she let him see how reluctant she'd been to come to England.

The removals and storage people had already arrived and were waiting to unload the furniture, and for the next few hours Giselle was kept busy, telling them where to put it, while her father wandered happily from room to room like a child with a new toy. But Abbeyfields wasn't new to him, was it? she thought. It was old and full of memories that he must have cherished over the years.

'I lived here with my parents until I married your mother,' he told her. 'When they died a distant cousin of mine bought the place. He and his wife have also passed on, and *I've* come home. But what about you, Giselle? I've been thinking only of myself. Are you going to be happy here?'

It had been a long day and she flashed him a tired smile. 'Yes, of course,' she assured him, and wished it was the truth.

Marc hadn't been wrong in thinking that his children would be disappointed that they weren't moving to Abbeyfields. There had been scowls from nine-year-old Tom when he told them, and Alice, a quick-thinking six-year-old, had said tearfully, 'We can play in the fields, though, can't we? There's lots of grass and it's very high. No one will see us.'

'I'm afraid not. That would be trespassing,' he'd told her, wishing that their mother was there to help comfort them. But Amanda, horse loving and reckless, had been thrown with fatal results while out riding two years ago, and the three of them were facing life without her, with the help of his kindly in-laws.

'I promise that I *will* find us a house where you will have lots of room to play, but I want it to be the surgery as well, so that I know where you are and what you're doing while I'm working. Which means that it will take time for me to find the right place.'

He'd seen the van outside on the day the new owners moved in and had caught a flash of long legs in tight jeans and glossy brown hair tied back from a face that he remembered distinctly from that day at the auction rooms.

His curiosity about her had been appeased by a chat with James Morrison from the garden centre, who had explained that Giselle Howard had bid for Abbeyfields on behalf of her father, who had lived there before he'd married a French woman and gone to live in Paris.

'You wouldn't remember him,' he'd been told. 'It was a long time ago, but Philip Howard and I have kept in touch and I'm afraid that you have me to blame for you not getting the house. I wrote and told him it was for sale and he decided to come back. Can't wait to get his foot over the doorstep, but I don't think Giselle is as keen as he is. She was happy where she was.'

So that was the story, Marc had thought, and somehow it made his disappointment regarding the house less painful.

The morning after they'd moved in to Abbeyfields Philip Howard wasn't well.

He had woken up with a severe headache and pain in the joints, and after she'd examined him Giselle rang James Morrison to say that her father was ill and was there a doctor in the village?

'Aye, of course there is,' was the reply. 'But you're one yourself, aren't you?'

'Yes, I am,' she told him. 'But I have no equipment with me apart from a stethoscope and some painkillers…and I *am* in a strange country. I think that Dad might just be suffering from over-exertion and excitement from yesterday, but I need to be sure.'

'It's just across the main street from where you are.' she was told. 'If you pop across now, you'll get one of the doctors before they start morning surgery.'

'I'm going to get a doctor,' she told her father. 'The surgery is just across the way. I need someone to check you over properly.'

It was a drab-looking place, Giselle thought as she pushed open the door of a building where the stonework was blackened with age, but only on the outside she discovered as she stepped into a bright, modern reception area, where a pleasant, middle-aged woman eyed her questioningly.

'My father and I moved into the village yesterday,' Giselle told her, 'and I'm afraid that we need a doctor. He isn't well this morning and I'd like someone to come out to him.'

The woman nodded.

'None of the doctors are here yet,' she said. 'It's only eight-fifteen and we don't start surgery until half past, but as soon as one of them arrives I will ask him to have a word with you.'

At that moment a car pulled up outside and the receptionist said, 'That sounds like Dr Bannerman now.'

Marc had been about to drop the children off at the school at the other end of the village when Tom had remembered that he should have taken his games kit. Leaving the children to go into assembly, Marc had gone back for it, thinking as he did so that mornings were the worst part of the day. Getting them up in time. Making sure they had a good breakfast and checking they'd got everything before leaving the house, which didn't seem to have worked very well that morning,

And now a busy day at the surgery was about to commence, with Craig absent as it was his day at college and a phone call just as he was getting out of bed to say that Stanley, his father-in-law, was ill with shingles that he thought he'd picked up from a patient.

As he came swinging through the door, pointing himself towards Reception, he called out, 'Any chance of a brew, Mollie? Tom forgot his games kit and I've just had to dash back for it. Talk about never a dull moment! I seem to remember having a piece of toast round about sevenish and that was it.'

The woman behind the desk smiled.

'Yes, of course, Doctor, and while I'm putting the kettle on, there's a lady to see you.'

'Oh?'

As he turned Giselle was rising to her feet in slow amazement as she took in the fact that the man from the auction was the local GP.

'Hello, there,' he said coolly. 'We meet again.'

'Yes,' she said uncomfortably. 'I am sorry to bother you so soon as we only moved in yesterday, but—'

'Yes, I know,' he said, breaking into her explanation, as if what he had to say was more important. 'I saw you.'

'You did?'

'Yes. I was driving past and saw the container truck outside.'

'Really? I'm sorry, but I do have to get back to my father. I'm here to ask if you would visit him. He isn't at all well this morning. He has a severe headache and pain in the joints.'

'I'll be over in ten minutes,' he said, and Giselle breathed a sigh of relief.

Firstly, because she was going to get another opinion, and secondly, because she would have a few moments to gather her wits.

'Thank you,' she said, and left him to his 'brew' and whatever else was going to take him ten minutes to accomplish.

When she'd gone Marc went into his consulting room and sank down into the chair behind his desk. He'd been wondering when they would meet again, but hadn't expected it to be so soon, and now he was going to set foot in the house that he'd hoped would one day be his.

This morning the elegant woman of the auction looked tired and washed out. She'd also been embarrassed and he didn't have to look far for the reason for that.

Mollie was putting a steaming mug in front of him and as he drank the hot tea thankfully he was already reaching for his bag and preparing to visit the intriguing Giselle and her father.

'I can't find anything wrong,' Marc said when he'd examined Philip. 'The headache could be from the stress of the move yesterday and the pain in the joints... Were you lifting any heavy stuff about during the move, Mr Howard?'

Giselle shook her head, but her father admitted sheepishly, 'I did shift a few things when my daughter wasn't looking.'

'That could be it,' he said. 'You've been using muscles that you don't normally use. But don't hesitate to send for me again if the problems persist.'

When he was ready to go and they were standing out of earshot in the high panelled hall, Giselle said awkwardly, 'I'm in health care myself, but thought I should get another opinion.'

'You are?'

'Er…yes. Until recently I was employed as a registrar in a Paris hospital.'

The deep blue gaze of the man standing opposite had widened.

'I'm sorry I sent for you,' she said, her face crumpling, afraid he thought she had wasted his time. 'It's just that I'm so tired and miserable I can't think straight. My father was so anxious to come back to this place that I can't bear the thought of anything denying him his dream.'

'And what about you? Was it your dream, too?' he asked.

She shook her head dolefully.

'No. I would have liked to have stayed in Paris. All my friends are there…and my job. But I can't leave my father. We buried my mother not so long ago and he needs me.'

'So you aren't looking forward to village life?'

'Not really, but I suppose I'll get used to it. I'll have to.'

'Is that why you were so on edge when we were bidding against each other?'

'Yes, partly. That, and a dread of failing in what I'd been sent to do. I knew that day how much you wanted this house and that I was taking it from you, and I've felt guilty ever since.'

Marc laughed. 'Good grief! You had no cause to. Business is business. Let the best man—or woman—win. It was just that we're so busy at the surgery I've been looking for a bigger place, ideally with living accommodation attached so that I'm not to-ing and fro-ing between my house and the practice all the time. And my kids were looking forward to playing in those rolling green fields at the back of here.'

Giselle smiled wryly. 'You are making me feel even worse.'

'There's no need. We'll find somewhere else.'

'So where is your wife?'

'Dead, I'm afraid,' he said abruptly. 'She was thrown from a horse and killed.'

'Oh, no! How awful,' she breathed.

He nodded.

'Yes, it was, but life is full of awful things, like having to come and live amongst the local yokels.'

She was smiling now.

'Dr Bannerman.'

'Yes? And it's Marc.'

'Your children are welcome to play in the fields at the back of Abbeyfields any time they like, as Dad and I aren't likely to be out there much. No need to ask permission. They can use the side gate.'

'That is very kind, and what do I call you? Dr Howard? Or Giselle?'

'Giselle, I think. It could be some time before I put on my white coat again.'

He was ready to leave, having visions of the waiting room filling up, but he had one last thing to say.

'It was nice to meet you properly…Giselle.

I hope that you won't be too disappointed with us when you get to know us.' And off he went, across the main street and into the practice with a lighter step than before.

As Giselle watched him go she was thinking that so far she couldn't answer for what she would think of the rest of them, but she was far from disappointed in Marc.

He was a man carrying a heavy load in all quarters, and she hoped that the next time they met she wouldn't be so drippish *and* would be looking smarter than today. And with that thought came another. When was she going to get the chance to wear all her smart outfits in this place?

Her father felt better as the day wore on and as Giselle carried on with arranging the inside of the house to accommodate their belongings, the conversation with Marc was uppermost in her mind.

He hadn't had much to say about his dead wife, she thought, but who could blame him for that? She shouldn't have asked, but she'd been curious about him from the moment she'd seen him sitting across from her at the auction, though she didn't know why.

A vision of Raoul came to mind, lording it in his boutique, and after talking to Marc Bannerman she didn't understand what she'd ever seen in the Frenchman.

What had the wholesome-looking GP thought about her? she wondered. A woman who thought she was above the villagers? She hoped not. Giselle wished that she hadn't told him how she'd been loth to move to the English countryside. He would think she was a moaner and a snob, and she was neither of those things.

CHAPTER TWO

HER father's aches and pains had disappeared by the following day and as a bright summer sun shone down on the village he went to visit his friends at the garden centre, keen to find his way around after his long absence.

He'd wanted Giselle to go with him but she'd given him a smiling refusal, guessing that he would like to make his first venture outside of Abbeyfields on his own. But he'd made her promise that she would meet up with him for lunch at the hotel standing on raised ground behind the dismal façade of the surgery.

She'd agreed reluctantly, not wanting another encounter with Marc as she felt that if he saw her father, hale and hearty, trotting about the place, he would think that she was some doctor, panicking over him like she had.

Although she would expect him to be aware that often after a bereavement those left behind felt that they, or someone else close to them, would soon be the next. That was certainly how she'd felt. After losing her mother, her father was doubly precious.

When she strolled past the surgery to keep the lunch date with her father, there was no sign of Marc and she hoped that was how it would stay.

Why did she feel she had to prove herself to him? she thought irritably. The odds were that they would rarely meet if he was so bogged down with the practice and his family.

Arriving at the hotel, Giselle saw that there was a leisure complex and gymnasium attached to it, and with the feeling that things were looking up in this rural retreat she decided to go inside and have a look around as she had time to spare before meeting her father.

When she stepped into the foyer she saw immediately that with regard to Marc Bannerman the fates were still pulling her strings. He was on his knees amongst the sofas and easy chairs, bending over the still form of a middle-aged man, with the manager of the complex hovering and a couple of the members looking on anxiously.

As if sensing her presence, he looked up from checking the man's pulse and called across, 'Giselle! You are a welcome sight. I suspect we have a cardiac arrest here. No heartbeat or pulse. We need to resuscitate.'

'Right,' she said dazedly, dropping to her knees at the other side of the man's still form. His skin was cold and clammy, his lips blue and his hair was damp on his brow, as if he'd recently been under the shower.

'I'll take the mouth-to-mouth while you do the compressions,' he said quickly.

She nodded. Her crossed hands were already pressing down on the man's chest. After the fifth compression Marc held the man's nose and placed his mouth over his while he gave one deep breath, then it was back to Giselle again.

They continued with the procedure.

The manager had been watching out for the ambulance that he'd sent for the moment the man had collapsed and now the cardiac arrest team arrived. Paramedics and a doctor were hurrying to the man's side and Marc quickly explained the situation.

'Right. We'll take it from here,' he was told. 'We'll do an ECG on the spot and see what that tells us.'

'Too much exercise maybe,' one of the paramedics said as he bent over the patient. 'Whatever the reason, he was lucky that the two of you were on hand. He would have gone to meet his maker by the time we got here.'

Giselle and Marc watched the ambulance drive off before going back inside to have a word with the manager.

'The guy comes in twice each week and uses the gym for a couple of hours,' the man said. 'He'd showered and was on his way out when he keeled over. Was I glad that you were on the premises, Dr Bannerman!'

Marc smiled. 'And I was equally relieved to see Dr Howard appear on the scene.' Turning to Giselle, he said, 'I was here, visiting this gentleman's wife. She's had a bad dose of summer flu and I've been keeping an eye on her.'

Still dazed by the whole thing, Giselle said, feeling that she was being called upon to explain her own presence, 'I was on my way to have lunch with my father in the hotel next door. I only came in for a brochure.'

'Which just goes to show that village life is not as dull as you expected,' Marc said with a smile, and she found herself smiling back.

'Maybe not,' she told him, 'but I can't stay to discuss that. My father will be wondering where I've got to.'

'Of course,' he agreed, 'but before you go, thanks for being here, Giselle.'

'It was my pleasure,' she said inanely, and immediately thought what a stupid thing to say. That kind of thing was always a nerve-racking experience, and meeting up with the village doctor so soon after telling herself that they probably wouldn't be seeing much of each other hadn't been all that much of a pleasure either, as she wanted to be left alone to find her own way in the new life that had been thrust upon her.

It was to be a strange day. In the late afternoon, while her father was having a rest after his earlier exertions, Giselle heard voices and childish laughter coming from the fields at the back of the house, and when she looked out she saw two bright splashes of colour amongst the uncut grasses.

She was smiling. It had to be the Bannerman children who had taken advantage of her offer with all speed, and she went out to introduce herself.

When Tom and Alice saw her approaching they became still and eyed her cautiously. Anxious to put them at ease, Giselle said, 'Hello, there.'

'Our dad said it was all right for us to come

and play here,' Tom said quickly, without re-turning her greeting.

'Yes, it is,' she told them. 'I told him you could. My name is Giselle. What's yours?'

'I'm Tom and she's Alice,' the boy said, pointing towards his sister who was observing her unblinkingly.

'So have you been to school today?'

It would seem that Alice had found her voice as she said, 'Yes. We went home to change and then came here.'

'Would you like a drink?'

'Yes, please,' they chorused.

'Milk or orange juice? I've only just moved here and there isn't much in the fridge.'

'We know you've just moved in,' Tom said. 'Dad wanted to buy this house, but he told us that a French lady with lots of money had bought it.'

Giselle winced. The guilty feeling was there again.

'It is my father who has bought it, not me,' she told them, 'and your dad is mistaken. I am only half-French and I haven't got a lot of money.'

Both statements were true. Especially the last. Soon she would have to look for employment, and if she found work in one of the big hospitals in the nearest town she would be leaving her father alone for many hours each day. He might have been buzzing around the village that morning, but he was exhausted now and only she knew how big a strain her mother's illness had been on him.

But there was no immediate rush to find work. It was a warm summer afternoon and Tom, who looked like his father with a fair mop and blue eyes, and Alice, who was brown-eyed and dark-haired like herself, drank a glass of milk and went back into the fields, having the time of their lives.

It was half past five when their father came to collect them, and he said briefly, 'Have they been good, Giselle?'

'They've been fine,' she told him.

He nodded and then said, 'I can't stop. I'm in the middle of the late afternoon surgery and have popped out to take the children round to my mother-in-law's for their evening meal, but I would like a word when it's convenient. Will you be free later this evening.'

Giselle almost laughed. She would be free all right, as apart from himself and the Morrisons she didn't know a soul in this place.

'Er...yes,' she said hesitantly, as she wondered what he could possibly want to discuss with her. She hoped it wasn't bad news about the heart attack victim from earlier in the day, but no doubt she would soon find out.

'I'll come round about sevenish, if that's all right. If I wait until the children are in bed, it will mean getting someone to babysit for me.'

'Er...yes,' she said again, as if possessed of a limited vocabulary. His manner was brisk and businesslike and she was behaving like a wet lettuce.

'The doctor who came to see you yesterday is coming round this evening,' she told her father when he came downstairs.

'But I'm all right now,' he said in mild protest.

Giselle smiled. 'He's coming to see me.'

'Really! Well, well!'

'He's a widower with two young children,' she told him, 'so don't get any wrong ideas.'

'Anyone would be better than that fellow in the dress shop,' he snorted. 'I don't know what you see in him.'

'*Saw* in him,' she corrected. 'Raoul is in the past.' She turned away to hide a smile at the thought of Raoul's elegant boutique being described as a 'dress shop'. The only thing that would annoy Raoul more would be if his expensive stock were to be described as 'frocks'.

Marc didn't seem quite so brisk when he came back later that evening. He was a man with a lot on his mind and was about to unload some of it onto a complete stranger, because that was what Giselle Howard was. Yet it didn't feel quite like that.

Their paths kept crossing, which wasn't surprising as the village was only a small place. But it was more than that. It was almost as if she'd been sent to relieve his burden and he was hoping that she would see it his way.

Giselle had unearthed a bottle of French wine from one of the packing cases still to be emptied and was prepared to do the hospitality routine. Her father had left them together after telling the local GP that he was feeling much better, and now, seated opposite Giselle in the pleasant sitting room that he'd thought one day might be his, Marc was about to amaze the woman sitting opposite him.

'I know you must be wondering why I've come,' he said.

'Yes, I am,' she said, feeling more composed now than when they'd spoken before. 'I can't possibly think what you could have to say to me, unless it's bad news about the heart-attack man.'

'No, not at all. I phoned the coronary unit this afternoon. He's responding to treatment. I suppose in a way he *is* connected with what I have to say, as what happened at the gym this morning put the idea into my head.'

Giselle was wishing he would come to the

point. He didn't give the impression of being a ditherer, but what was he on about?

'I've just come from my in-laws' house, where my wife's father is quite ill with shingles. He is one of the mainstays of the practice, though he should have retired years ago, and observing him now I can't see him coming back. But that is something for future consideration. It is the present that concerns me at the moment.'

'Yes, I'm sure that it does,' she murmured, and wondered why he was unburdening himself to her, of all people.

'So I'm here to ask if you would be interested in helping me out at the surgery on a temporary basis.'

She was shaking her head before he'd even finished speaking. 'I don't think so. I don't know anyone here,' she said quickly, before he could say anything else. 'From the little I've seen of the place, it's somewhere where everyone knows everyone else, and I don't think a strange doctor would be welcome.'

It was a weak excuse. She knew it. But it was all she could think of at that moment. He had taken her completely by surprise, though she could see the logic in his thinking. She was a doctor, at present unemployed, and living in the village. But this surprising man seemed to have forgotten that she'd told him that she hadn't wanted to leave France. How miserable she was here. She thought she'd made it clear that she couldn't see herself mixing with the locals, and here he was, asking her to do that very thing.

Marc, surprised by the degree of his disappointment, put the empty wineglass down on a small table at his elbow and got to his feet. He understood her reluctance. Giselle was from a very different background to his. She'd been brought up in one of the most famous cities in the world and now found herself in a small close-knit community that must seem claustrophobic by comparison.

'What the people here want with regard to the practice are good doctors,' he said, looking down on her. 'Whether they have known those treating them since they were only knee-high or have never set eyes on them before isn't important.'

'But how do you know that *I* would be any good?' she questioned. 'Just because I teamed up with you at the gymnasium, it doesn't mean I would make a satisfactory GP.'

'Obviously not. I'm relying on instinct. But that doesn't mean I wouldn't be asking for career details and wanting to know if you've done any GP work before. Also, I would have to get in touch with the primary care trust here and the health authorities across the Channel.'

Giselle was rallying. She felt as if she was being pushed into a corner by this busy doctor she hardly knew. Was he always as forceful as this? she wondered. He had commandeered her services at the gymnasium and she'd no quarrel with that as it had been a desperate situation that she'd walked into, but now he was trying to organise her life.

He didn't know that at the back of her mind

was the thought that if her father regained some of his vigour, and his happiness at coming back to his roots didn't diminish, she might go back to Paris in a few months' time if she felt that he could manage without her.

She sympathised with Marc's predicaments, both of them, the situation at the practice and his responsibilities to his motherless children, but those were his problems, not hers.

She shook her head again.

'I would rather you found someone else. Surely there are locums available for such situations as you find yourself in? Or trainees required to do some GP work as part of their course?'

'I've already got one of those,' he said, 'but making any other kind of arrangement takes time, and knowing my father-in-law he'll be getting up out of his sickbed and reporting for duty if he knows I'm pushed.'

He didn't know why he wasn't taking no for an answer. Was it because having this fellow doctor with the piquant face and wary violet eyes around the surgery would make life more livable? If it was, she would be the first woman he'd looked at as a person since Amanda had died.

But short of getting down on his knees, he didn't see what else he could do, so he said, 'I'm sorry. I'm keeping you from whatever you had planned for tonight and I have to get back to my family. Thank you for your time, Giselle.' And without further comment he went.

He had referred to what she might have planned for tonight, she thought disbelievingly when he'd gone. Had it been sarcasm? A reminder that with so little going on in her life, a job at the practice was not to be sneezed at?

'So what did the good doctor want?' her father asked when he reappeared, and Giselle was immediately aware that she musn't let him know just how homesick she was.

'He came to ask if I would like to work in the practice,' she said casually.

Bushy brows above grey eyes were rising.

'Really! And what did you say?'

'Er…I said no. That it was too early to take up that sort of commitment.'

'It would be one way of getting to know the people round here,' he said, echoing Marc's comment, and she turned away. She knew that. Didn't have to be told. But she wasn't exactly yearning for that to happen, was she? She'd accepted that she'd come to live in this place, but it didn't mean that she was going to become a local.

Her father was still saying his piece and it was to the effect that her skills were going to be wasted if she didn't go back into health care.

'I know that, *papa*,' she told him gently, 'but what if I would rather be back in a big hospital than a village surgery?'

'The choice is up to you, my dear,' he said peaceably, 'whenever you are ready to make the decision. And now, after a long look at the glorious peaks, I'm going to bed.'

He kissed her gently on the brow and, adding to her confusion, said, 'Wherever you decide to take up your career again, don't let it be too far away. The days will be long without you.'

When he'd gone she groaned softly. What wouldn't she give to be sailing along the Seine, with a silver moon above and Raoul beside her, selfish and arrogant though he might be? The only waterway she'd seen in these parts was the murky-looking canal that ran past the back of the surgery.

She climbed the stairs at last with her resolve unchanged, but as she lay sleepless beneath the covers her thoughts wouldn't let her rest. For some reason the children kept coming to mind. Tom and Alice. They were cute and looked well cared-for, but it was on the cards that they wouldn't see much of their remaining parent, and if he was going to be a doctor short, they would see even less of him.

Added to that, her father's words kept coming back and they made sense. If she found work locally she wouldn't be spending time travelling to and from wherever she was employed, which would increase the time she was away from him. And more important, if he needed her, she would be within easy reach.

Are you on the point of changing your mind because of the man, the money or the thought of long, endless days with nothing to break the monotony? she asked herself as dawn banished the summer dark.

There could be another reason, of course. She'd already been on a guilt trip because they'd bought the house from under Marc's nose, and now she was feeling even more guilty by refusing to help out at the practice.

The next day was Saturday. The children had gone out for the day with the mother of one of Tom's friends and as Marc went to take the short morning surgery before the weekend began, Giselle wasn't the only one questioning their motives.

It was true that they were really pushed at the practice without Stanley, he thought but, as Giselle had pointed out as she'd tried to conceal her dismay at his suggestion, he could have soon got a replacement. But he wanted her there, didn't he? She intrigued him.

There'd been a few women in his life since he'd lost Amanda. He supposed he was a catch up to a point, but if he was, he was a catch with two young children and he would be very careful if he ever decided to replace their mother.

Amanda had been one of the Cheshire set, into golf and hunting, and would have preferred him to be as sporty as she, but a country practice took some looking after and though she'd been a faithful wife and loving mother, they hadn't always agreed on their priorities.

He was smiling as he pulled up in front of the surgery. The woman who'd refused his suggestion the previous night was no lookalike. Small-boned and petite, with dark glossy hair that she either wore swept back off her face or left to hang free, she was the exact opposite of his dead wife, who had possessed her own attractions, but in a much more ample sort of way.

There was only one receptionist on duty on

Saturday mornings and it seemed as if she had still to arrive as there were no signs of life around the place. As he reached for his keys Marc was aware of someone watching him from the shadows of the porch, and as she stepped forward his heart skipped a beat.

'Giselle!' he exclaimed, as she moved into the light.

'Good morning, Dr Bannerman,' she said quietly. 'Would we have time for a word before surgery starts?'

'Yes, by all means,' he said with a smile that was taking note of legs in tailored trousers, with a crisp cotton shirt hanging above them and, annoyingly, eyes hidden behind dark glasses.

He led the way into his consulting room and motioned for her to take a seat. 'So?' he said. 'Have you come to complain about me interfering in the life that you want to keep so private?'

'No,' she told him, with assumed calm. 'I've come to say that I've changed my mind. I will help out at the surgery if you still want me to.'

'That *is* good news,' he said, with his eyes on the mouth that had just said the words he wanted to hear. It was a kind mouth, a sensitive one, and yet he sensed that Giselle would be no walk-over if she dug her heels in.

'What has made you change your mind?' he asked.

'Not any one thing,' she told him. 'There are a few reasons, which I prefer not to discuss.'

'Fine,' he said easily. 'Just as long as you are coming to join us here. We usually only get a smattering of patients on Saturday mornings, so if you would like to have a look around while I'm dealing with them and maybe have a chat with Mollie, who is the receptionist on duty today, we can continue our discussion afterwards.'

Giselle nodded and got to her feet, and as he escorted her into the reception area, where Mollie was just taking off her coat, he said, 'Look after Dr Howard, will you, Mollie? I am hoping that she will soon be joining us.'

* * *

'I did some general practice work before I went on to the wards,' Giselle told him when Mollie had left and they were back in his consulting room. 'I can give you details of that and where I got my degree. I was a registrar on the gynae-cological wards for three years at a hospital in Paris until I took time off to nurse my mother. I'd been looking forward to going back, but had to give in my notice when my father decided that he wanted to come back to England.'

Marc nodded. 'I can see why you're not over the moon with your present circumstances, but I can assure you of one thing—the village's female population will welcome you with open arms, especially if you've been on the women's wards. I will e-mail everyone I can to get the formalities over as quickly as possible, and in the meantime look forward to seeing you on Monday morning, if that's all right with you.'

'Yes, it will be all right,' she agreed, 'and if any problems do arise about my suitability, I won't mind stepping down.'

'You sound as if you wouldn't be too upset if that happened,' he remarked dryly, and knew that if she wouldn't mind, *he* would.

'Maybe,' she told him, 'but there is the other side to it. Helping you out might ease my conscience a little.'

'What has your conscience got to do with it?'

'Your disappointment and that of your children because you didn't get the house is still on my mind, and if my not accepting your offer of employment means they'll see less of you, I'll feel even worse.'

He observed her with surprised blue eyes. 'You've no cause to feel guilty about anything with regard to myself and my children,' he said in a tone that was cooling. 'I am quite capable of understanding that you had your own priorities to think about.'

'And *I* am quite capable of realising that maybe you feel sorry for me, finding myself in a strange place amongst strangers,' she parried.

'Nothing of the kind,' he said, as the atmosphere continued to deteriorate. 'My motives are selfish. I need some help and presumably you need employment, so shall we leave it at that?'

He was getting to his feet, indicating that the discussion was at an end. Giselle did likewise, with the feeling that the process of getting to know each other had just taken a couple of backward steps.

'Until Monday morning, then,' he said, holding out his hand. As she extended her own, Giselle knew that she was going to like his touch. It was as she'd expected. There was nothing of the wet fish about Marc's hand-shake. It was firm and confident. The clasp of a man who was quite capable of sorting out his own affairs without the misplaced sympathy of a neurotic misfit.

Instead of going straight back to Abbeyfields, Giselle decided to make her first visit to the shops. There weren't many of them. A spotlessly clean butcher's, a chemist, ladies' and gents' hairdressers, a baker's with a display of wholesome-looking cakes and pastries and, twice the size of the rest, a combined general store and post office.

'You'll be the young woman who's moved into Abbeyfields, no doubt,' the elderly woman behind the counter in the baker's shop said chattily, as Giselle bought a big crusty loaf and a fruit cake.

'Er, yes, I am,' she replied evasively, and left it at that, but she wasn't going to escape so easily.

'I'm told that it's Philip Howard who has bought the place. Would you be his daughter?'

'Yes, I am,' she admitted reluctantly, uncomfortable that they were being discussed to such an extent.

'Well, tell him that Jenny Goodwin sends her regards. We were in the same class at school. Take him one of these, for old times' sake.' And she picked up a large Bakewell tart and placed it beside Giselle's other purchases.

'That's very kind of you,' Giselle said, taken aback.

'Think nothing of it,' she was told. 'You've

just lost your ma, haven't you? That must have been hard.'

'Yes, it was terrible,' she admitted, and couldn't believe that she was discussing her innermost feelings with this sympathetic elderly woman. Amazing herself even more, she went on to say, 'We lived in Paris. My mother was French.'

'Yes. I well remember your father bringing this beautiful French girl to meet his parents. In no time at all they were married.'

Giselle could feel a lump in her throat. That was a part of her father's life that she knew nothing about, and it was incredible that she'd met someone who remembered her mother.

She had to get out of there before she broke down and wept. 'Thank you for the pastry,' she said, as she turned to go.

'What's your name?' the woman behind the counter asked.

'Giselle.'

'Well, Giselle, it's been lovely to meet you. Anytime you feel like a chat, pop round. It takes a bit of getting used to when you move to somewhere new, doesn't it?'

'Yes, it does,' she choked, and went before she made a spectacle of herself.

But as she walked the short distance back to the house Giselle found herself smiling. Jenny Goodwin was a nice homely woman. If the rest of the village people were like her *and* the doctor who seemed to be everywhere she turned, then life there might not be as dull as she'd imagined.

When he saw the Bakewell tart and heard who'd sent it, her father's face lit up. 'Jenny Goodwin!' he exclaimed. 'I remember her well. We used to go scrumping together.'

'What is that?'

'Looking for apples that have fallen off the trees at harvest-time, and sometimes, when the owners weren't looking, giving them a helping hand,' he told her laughingly. 'We were chased out of the fields and gardens many a time.'

'She remembered *maman*.'

He nodded.

'Yes. I can imagine that she would, as Jenny and I might have got together if I hadn't met Celeste. It would seem that she never got around to tying the knot herself if she is still called Goodwin.'

That was the difference in this place, Giselle thought as she gazed at the rugged skyline from her bedroom window that night. The people who lived here weren't just faces and voices on a Paris street. They were a community who cared about each other. Which, she supposed, could be seen as interference sometimes. But they would be good to have around in a time of need, and as she drifted off to sleep in the quietness that she still found so strange after the bustle of the city, she didn't feel quite so lost and lonely.

CHAPTER THREE

WHEN Giselle awoke on Monday morning the first thought that came into her mind was the promise she'd made to Marc. As she watched the morning sun dappling the ceiling of her bedroom it was a strange feeling, knowing that she had somewhere to go, something to do, besides the endless task of unpacking their belongings.

Maybe a lack of purpose had been one of the reasons for her melancholy, she thought, and the village doctor had done her a favour by suggesting that she stand in for his ailing father-in-law. She'd seen shingles a few times and at its worst it could be a very nasty and painful illness, especially if the blisters were on the face and head. She'd actually seen a patient die from it when the severity of it had caused meningitis. Giselle hoped that nothing so awful was going to happen in this instance, as she would be reminding Marc from time to time that she was only filling in for his father-in-law, not replacing him.

When she arrived at the surgery there were three cars on the forecourt, but none of them was the one that Marc had arrived in on Saturday morning. It looked as if he was still on the school run.

A young man in a suit, shirt and tie was hovering in Reception, and as he eyed her appreciatively he introduced himself as Craig Richards, the trainee GP. He handed her over to a smiling Mollie, who asked if she would like a cup of tea before the action began.

She could feel the tension that had gripped her ever since getting out of bed lessening as she accepted the offer, and while the kettle was coming up to the boil Mollie introduced her to the rest of the staff. There were three receptionists and two nurses, and a smart, middle aged woman who had only just arrived turned out to be the practice manager.

Giselle was standing by the reception desk, sipping the tea, when the door opened and the man who had been on her mind all weekend came in.

Since they'd spoken on Saturday Marc hadn't had a moment to spare. While the children had been out for the day he'd done the washing and ironing and cut the often neglected lawns around his house, so that he would have Sunday free to be with Tom and Alice.

The rest of the household chores were done by a cleaning lady who came in twice each week. That was how they survived, with Margaret, his wonderful mother-in-law, having himself and the children round each weekday for their evening meal.

It was working. The children were happy and contented, apart from the odd moments when they missed their mother. Such as when Alice had begged to go to a dancing class held in the church hall and it had been Grandma who'd had to take her instead of Mummy. And when Tom had cut his leg badly after a fall off his skateboard, he'd cried for his mum.

Marc could never gauge correctly how much *he* missed Amanda. There had been times when he'd thought her selfish when she'd gone galloping off on one of her own pursuits, but she'd always been there to pick up the children from school and had a meal of sorts ready when he'd arrived home after a busy day at the practice. They'd jogged along happily enough, but he hadn't been madly in love. Occasionally he missed her ample curves in his bed at night, but more often than not he was too tired to even think about anything other than sleep.

It hadn't been like that over the weekend, though. He'd been tired enough when he'd gone to bed, but sleep had evaded him and it had all been because of the woman who was observing him warily from beside the reception desk. Every time he'd closed his eyes her face had been there, the creamy skin, high cheekbones…and kissable mouth.

'Hello, there, Giselle,' he said, flashing her a smile. 'Have you been introduced to everyone?'

She nodded 'Yes. Thank you.'

As Mollie passed him a mug of tea his smile switched to her and he said, 'Thanks, Mollie. I'm ready for this. Monday mornings are the worst.' Almost in the same breath he went on, 'Right, let's get started. Can someone check if the test results for Richard Benyon are back? I'm due to see him this morning.' He turned to Giselle. 'I'd like you to sit in with me today. It will give you the chance to see how we function.'

'Yes. Whatever you say,' she agreed, not sure if she wanted such close proximity so soon.

'Maisie, this is Dr Howard,' he said to his first patient, a crochety-looking elderly woman. 'She is here as a temporary replacement for Dr Pollard.'

'Yes, I've heard.' And as a pair of old eyes

surrounded by wrinkles looked Giselle over, she said, 'I'm told that you're from over there.'

Giselle didn't reply and Marc cast a quick glance in her directon. The last thing he wanted was for her to discover that she was being talked about. But his first patient of the day was already moving on to another subject and asking abruptly, 'So Is Stanley no better, then?'

Giselle hid a smile. She could imagine the expressions on the faces of the doctors in a large hospital if the patients were so familar.

'No. I'm afraid not,' Marc told her gravely.

Giselle's amusment increased when Maisie said, 'So he wouldn't be able to manage one of my steak and kidney puddings if I made him one.'

He shook his head. 'It is a nice thought, but I wouldn't trouble yourself as he's eating very little.'

'All right. Maybe another time, then,' she said, and went into a list of her ailments. He let her ramble on for a few minutes and then interrupted by saying, 'Most of the things that are causing you distress are from pain in the joints, Maisie. Have you been taking the medication that I prescribed for you last week.'

'Er…aye…when I remember.'

'You *must* take it. Get one of those long pill boxes where you can put a dose for each day inside. If you do that you'll soon know if you've forgotten to take your tablets. I'm going to send you for a bone scan,' he went on, and as she pursed her lips and observed him from beneath lowered brows he explained, 'It's standard procedure these days for older women, so don't get alarmed.'

'What is it for?'

'To check for signs of osteoporosis.'

'And where do I have to go?'

'Manchester University.'

As she opened her mouth to protest Marc told her, 'I know what you're going to say, but don't worry about transport. An ambulance will take you there and bring you back.'

Maisie sighed. 'All right, if you say so.' She got up off the chair slowly. 'Is that all, then?'

'No. I want to check your blood pressure while you're here, Maisie, so roll up your sleeve, please.'

When the old lady had gone, he turned to Giselle and she saw that he was smiling widely, displaying even white teeth. He had a firm mouth and a strong jawline, she thought. Out of the blue Raoul's face came to mind, handsome but in a petulant, sensual sort of way. The two men were so unalike they might have come from different planets.

Still smiling, he said, 'Maisie's heart is in the right place, but she has been known to come in from weeding the garden and put her hands straight into flour, so most of us try to avoid her home cooking.' Then, with his expression sobering, he said, 'I'm sorry about the interest your arrival in the village is causing, but the people here mean nothing hurtful by it. They are a close community and look after their own.'

'Exactly,' she said, 'but *I'm* not one of their own, and I *do* value my privacy. Remember, I'm not living here by choice.'

He nodded and she sensed that some of the buoyancy he'd been displaying had left him, but he was out to make a point.

'You say that you aren't one of us, but that isn't so. You are your father's daughter and he lived here once.'

He watched her expression soften. 'Yes. I suppose you're right. I'm afraid you'll have to give me time. I had a lovely chat with the lady at the baker's on Saturday. Incredibly, she remembered my mother and *that* helped to make me feel more as if I belonged.'

'Good,' he said briskly. 'And now, after Maisie, we have someone very different. Richard Benyon has multiple sclerosis. He has just regained his sight after losing it for a couple of weeks, which as we both know is one of the hazards of the illness when it affects the optic nerve.'

'How long has he had MS?'

'Eighteen years, and he's coped marvellously up to now, but this losing his sight business has shattered his confidence, as one might expect, and to say that he is depressed would be putting it mildly.'

The tall, sallow-complexioned man who seated himself opposite observed Giselle with little interest when Marc introduced her. 'Hi,' he said flatly, and then switched his glance to the man by her side. 'So what bad news have you got for me today, Marc? Is it going to happen again, and when?'

'Rick, you know that's a question I can't answer,' Marc told him. 'MS is such an unpredictable illness. Your sight could be affected again in a month from now, or it could be years, or even never, before it happens again. The corticosteroid drugs that you're on should help, but I can't make any promises that it won't happen again.'

'What about the MRI scan I had last week?'

'The results are back and they did show some signs of deterioration but, Rick, it could be so much worse. Your bladder isn't affected, as lots of people's are with the illness. Your limbs are still in good working order. I can imagine how desperate you felt while you couldn't see, but thank goodness your sight has come back.' Marc smiled. 'You've always been a positive thinker so don't let what has happened make you lose confidence. You owe it to Cassie and the children.'

The man at the other side of the desk smiled at last. 'I couldn't exist without them. How Cassie puts up with me, I really don't know.'

'Maybe it's because she loves you,' Marc told him. 'I'd like to see you again next week and if you're still feeling low I'll prescribe something to ease the depression.'

'I feel better from just having talked to you,' Richard said. Taking note of Giselle for the first time, he told her, 'This guy is the tops. He listens to other people's problems all day. I wonder who he tells about his.'

He's told *me* for one, she thought. Amongst all these people that he knows so well, he's told me.

When Richard had gone, Marc said, 'Richard is a solicitor with offices in the city. He has a lovely wife and children and rarely moans about the MS, but he is also a gifted artist and the thought of being prevented from doing something that means so much to him must have been totally depressing. Thankfully he's had a reprieve, but I couldn't tell him for how long.'

When surgery was over, Craig accosted Marc and asked in a low voice, 'Is Giselle doing the house calls with one of us?'

'Yes,' he was told.

'I'd like to volunteer.'

'I'll bet you would,' Marc said laughingly. 'But Dr Howard is with me today. Maybe in a few days' time, when she's got the hang of how we function, you can do the calls together.'

'Lucky you,' his assistant said enviously, and Marc's amusement increased, though he supposed that Craig had a point. It would be nice to have Giselle beside him as he visited those in the immediate vicinity requiring his attention, and others like them who lived in the more remote areas.

'So what did you think of your first morning with us?' Marc asked Giselle as he pulled out of the car park and headed towards their first call. 'Was it as bad as you expected?'

'Not quite,' she told him, thinking that he must see her as critical, as well as reclusive. 'Obviously it's very different from what I've been used to. I've never seen patients so relaxed with their doctor.'

Marc took his glance off the road for a moment and, looking across at her, couldn't help but notice the slender column of her throat rising out of the smart white silk blouse she'd chosen to wear for her first day as a country GP. He was gripped by sudden misgivings.

Was Giselle going to be a misfit at the surgery? Had he been so intrigued by her that he'd thrown common sense to the winds?

'And is that good or bad, do you think?' he asked.

It was Giselle's turn to look at him and there was surprise in *her* glance.

'Good, of course! How could it not be. You are unique,' she told him, remembering

Raoul, whose life was made up of socialising and sequins.

As soon as she'd said it, Giselle wished she hadn't. There were various ways that Marc could interpret the comment. She hoped he wouldn't read anything into it, other than admiration of him as a doctor.

He was smiling, and without reference to her last remark he said, 'That's a relief, then. To know that we've passed the test. I'm really glad to have you with us, Giselle, and a lot of our female patients will be, too. We've been short of a woman in the practice. They'll welcome you with open arms.'

He was pulling up beside one of the cottages on the main street and before they got out of the car he said, 'I feel that with this patient I am dealing with the baffling and often irritating Munchausen's syndrome. Irene Jackson is unmarried and lives alone. She nursed her mother, who had Parkinson's disease, for many years and since she died Irene seems to have taken on her mother's role of invalid, with a succession of ailments not proven. Irene has been admitted to hospital a few times and it has always turned out to be attention-seeking. Imaginary illnesses or self-inflicted injury.

'The thing that troubles me is that one day it might turn out like the boy who kept crying wolf. Anyway, today Irene is supposed to be suffering from tremors in the arms and legs.'

'Similar symptoms to Parkinson's disease,' Giselle commented.

'Exactly. Though her ailments do vary a lot. The only thing I can do for the poor woman is to try and protect her from unnecessary surgery or treatment. I've tried to get her to see someone regarding her mental state but she won't hear of it as I don't think she wants a cure. Her life revolves around her imaginary ailments.'

'That is so sad.'

'Yes. it is,' he agreed. 'So let's go and see what Irene has for us today,'

Before they could get out of the car the

front door was flung open and a small, middle aged woman with long straggly hair stood on the doorstep.

'How much longer are you going to stay out there?' she cried. 'I need to be taken to hospital.'

'Well, we'll just have to see about that, won't we, Irene?' Marc said gently as they followed her into an untidy sitting room. 'I've brought Dr Howard with me today. Shall we let her have a look at you first?'

'Not if she isn't going to send me to hospital.'

'We can't do that until we know there is something wrong with you.'

Giselle stepped forward to soothe the protesting woman. 'I'll sound your heart first,' she suggested, 'and then we'll check your blood pressure.'

When she'd finished, Giselle gave her patient a reassuring smile. 'Nothing wrong there,' she said gently. 'Now, show me where the tremors are.'

'In my arms and legs and if you don't send

for an ambulance you will be to blame if I die,' Irene snapped.

'Yes, well, maybe if I gave you something to make you a little calmer, you might feel better,' Giselle tried.

'I don't want to be calmer!' the woman wailed. 'I need surgery.'

'I don't think so,' Giselle told her firmly. 'What you need is a change of scene. Do you mix with other people much?'

'Of course I don't! I'm very sick. If you don't send me to hospital, I'll do something to myself.'

Giselle glanced across at Marc for guidance. So far he hadn't interrupted but now, seeing that she had come up against a dead end with the neurotic Irene, he knew that he couldn't take any chances. He was going to do what he'd done countless times before. If he left Irene here alone, there was no telling what she would do to herself. The hospital knew her, wouldn't be surprised to see her and would, no doubt, send her home once she'd been looked at. That having been done, the attention she'd received would satisfy her for a few weeks.

'I'm going to do as you ask,' he told her, 'but, Irene, you really do need to get out more, find other things to occupy your mind besides your aches and pains.'

Irene drew herself up to her full height. 'How often do I have to tell you, Dr Bannerman, that I am a sick woman?'

'You have already told me quite a few times and I have noted it down. I am now going to send for the ambulance but I feel you should know that they might start charging you for calling them out so often.'

The woman sniffed. 'Not when I'm so poorly they won't.'

There had been sighs all round when the paramedics had seen who they'd been called out to, but they'd done what they'd been asked to do and had taken her to A and E, and now the two doctors were about to carry on with their home visits.

As they drove away from the cottage Marc said, 'I feel that Irene's problem is that she saw so much illness with her mother, who was always the centre of attention because she was so ill, that when she died her daughter decided that it was time she had a turn.'

Giselle nodded. 'I noticed the *British Medical Encyclopaedia* on the window-sill. It's very sad and I wasn't exactly a success with my first woman patient, was I?'

'Irene was a one-off.' he told her. 'There won't be many like that. We're going up onto the moors now and my next patient can see us driving up the hill from his window, so the kettle will be on when we get there. He hasn't sent for me, but I call to see him from time to time without being asked. Frank Fairbank was injured in an accident with a tractor and is now disabled. He lost a leg and though he has a prosthesis he finds it difficult to get around. He has a small farm that his son has to run on his own now. The two men jog along all right, but I know how much the old man misses being active.'

His face was sombre as he went on to explain, 'It was Frank who found Amanda after the horse threw her. It was before his accident and he was out in one of the far fields when he came across the horse wandering around riderless. When he searched around he found her lying dead in a ditch.'

'Oh! That's awful,' she breathed.

'Yes. It wasn't good,' he agreed, and she could tell by the tone of his voice that he wasn't going to say anything further about Amanda.

When they pulled up outside the farmhouse, Toby, Frank's son, came round from the back and called, 'Hello, there, Dr Bannerman. My dad is in the kitchen, making the tea, He saw you coming.'

Marc smiled. 'That's what we want to hear. This is Dr Howard, Toby,' he said. 'She has just joined the practice. Stanley's got shingles and he's not at all well.'

'Pleased to meet you, Dr Howard,' the farmer's son said, looking slightly dazed. Marc thought that these two, father and son, wouldn't see many women up here in their all-male stronghold, especially one as attractive as Giselle Howard.

His father had come limping out to join them and when he had also been introduced his son said, 'Make sure you tell the doctor about your problem, Dad.'

'And what might that be?' Marc asked. 'You were fit as a fiddle the last time I called. Let's go inside, Frank, and you can tell me all about it.'

'I've got a lump in my groin. I think it's either cancer or a hernia,' the old farmer said once he'd led them into a cosy sitting room.

'There is a quite different degree of serious-ness between the two, I hope you know,' Marc told him whimsically. 'Anyway, let me have a look,'

'I'll wait in the other room,' Giselle said, aware that the older man hadn't been expect-ing her to arrive on the scene and might prefer to be alone with his GP. But he didn't seem bothered.

'There's no need,' Frank said. 'I'm sure you've seen it all before.'

'I can tell you what it isn't,' Marc told him when he'd examined him, 'but I can't tell you what it *is*. It is not a hernia.' He turned to Giselle. 'Would you like to give an opinion, Dr Howard?'

'I agree with you,' she said. 'It isn't a hernia. It might be a growth or a benign cyst, or it could be from the pressure of your prosthesis as it fits almost into the groin.'

Marc nodded his agreement and, turning to the elderly farmer, he said, 'I'll arrange for you to have some tests, Frank.'

'What sort?' the old man wanted to know.

'The usual. Blood tests, X-rays.'

'All right. How soon?'

'As soon as I can arrange it,' Marc told him, 'and in the meantime try not to worry.' As they turned to go he said, 'One last thing. How long have you had the lump, Frank?'

'A week or two.'

'Supposing I hadn't called. Would you have phoned the surgery?'

'I might have done if you hadn't shown up.'

Marc sighed. 'Might have done! You should have come to see me straight away.'

As they left the farm Marc said, 'Frank is a tough old guy. When he lost his leg there was no one about and he was trapped under the tractor for hours. Toby had gone for supplies and he found him there when he came back.'

'Do you think he *would* have come to the surgery?' Giselle asked.

'No, I don't. So it is fortunate that we called. I'll sort out an appointment the moment I get back, and in the meantime what do you want to do about lunch? It's almost one o'clock. There's an old inn up here where they serve good food. We could have a quick bite to sustain us, if you like.'

She didn't reply immediately and he thought that he was pushing it a bit. It was her first day in the practice. Giselle had hardly had time to get her breath and he was suggesting they have lunch together. Was he going to find himself in a situation where a woman had walked into his life and he couldn't stop thinking about her? How much of his asking for her help had been motivated because he was keen to have her near?

'Yes, that would be nice,' she said, and his spirits lifted. They would only have time for coffee and a sandwich, but at least he would have her to himself for a little while.

'Tell me about the children,' Giselle said as they seated themselves in a dining area near the bar.

Marc smiled. 'What do you want to know?'

'Anything. Their likes and dislikes. How they're getting on at school.'

'Tom will eat anything when it comes to food. Alice is harder to please. At school she is the clever one. Tom just plods along.'

'They must miss their mother.'

'Not as much as they did at first. Children soon accept change, but the scars of child-hood never go away. I do all I can to make up for her absence and most of the time it works.

but we do have our moments, I'm afraid. On the up side, Amanda's parents are very supportive. They've had their own grief to cope with but have kept it away from the children and are always there when we need them.'

As they chatted Marc thought that Giselle was the only woman he'd met who was more interested in his children than in him. He knew it wasn't an act. She'd already met them briefly and wanted to know more. He could have stayed and talked longer if they'd had the time.

She was looking around her at the grandeur of the peaks and the moors stretching into the sunlit skyline. 'It's very different to Paris, isn't it?' he said.

'Yes, it is,' she agreed, 'but it's very beautiful in its own way. I still can't get used to the quietness. No traffic noises at night, just the odd plane going over. At home there was always something to break the silence. We lived in a beautiful apartment by the river. My parents had been there ever since I was two years old.

'Celeste, *ma mère*, came from Paris and she

was homesick here. My father moved to his company's French office so that she could return to France. I took leave from my job to help him nurse her through cancer, and when she died I expected to go back, but my father took my breath away by saying he wanted to come back here. Because he was tired and lonely, I came with him.'

'And how do you feel about the move now?'

'Better. I have met you, and your patients, and the lady in the baker's shop who remembered my mother.'

So he was just one of a few, Marc thought wryly. Not the shining star amongst the clouds in her sky. But at least she wasn't shutting him out. Giselle was the best thing that had happened to him in years. Not just since he'd lost Amanda, but from before that. Their marriage had gone stale. They'd been almost living separate lives.

When she'd got the children ready for school each morning, she'd left him to see them safely inside and then she would be off to pick up Juniper, the frisky chestnut that she kept at stables in the village.

At night when he came home after a busy day at the practice she was almost invariably ready to go out, with the children bathed and fed and in their pyjamas and a meal for him in the oven. He'd got past caring where she went, but knew it would either be the bridge club, the gym or to the pub with her women friends.

He had been prepared to endure, remembering the vows he'd made on their wedding day and ever having the children's welfare at heart, but he'd not been happy.

The way it had ended had been the last thing he had ever imagined happening, and with freedom had come pain, grief and a huge feeling of responsibility.

Giselle was watching him with the amazing violet eyes that had attracted him from the start, and he thought that she would back off faster than the speed of light if she knew what he was thinking.

She was here beside him now because she'd

beaten him in the bidding for Abbeyfields and had felt guilty ever since. He was the last person *she* would ever look at under other circumstances. A widower with two children who never had a moment to spare. But what about now? He was finding time now, wasn't he?

This was pleasant, Giselle thought. Just the two of them for a little while. She felt comfortable with this man, more than she'd ever been with anyone in her life, especially Raoul. He'd been sensual and unpredictable and she'd enjoyed the excitement of it, but after the way he'd ended their relationship she never wanted to see him again.

She was surprised to find how much she was enjoying being involved in rural health care. At first, seeing patients in Marc's consulting room had seemed a bit claustrophobic after the large airy wards of a big hospital. But it was something she would soon get used to, and as for the patients they were like sick people everywhere, except that those she'd met today, with the exception of the Munchausen's lady, had a stoicism all their own.

The solicitor with MS. The elderly Maisie, who though a trifle crochety and plagued with rheumatism, had been concerned for the sick Stanley. But topping the list had been Frank, the farmer, with his artificial leg and the lump that he'd only mentioned because his GP had paid him a surprise visit.

Marc's glance was on her and she smiled across at him. 'I never dreamt when I came here that the fates would relent and send you to lift me out of my doldrums.'

'Does that mean you've decided that we aren't too boring after all?' he questioned as his heartbeat quickened.

'Yes. *I* am the one who's been boring, full of my own woes and so sorry for myself.'

'Nothing of the kind,' he told her firmly, and, pushing his chair back, he got to his feet. 'I regret to say that we need to be off. It will soon be time for the waiting room to fill up again.'

CHAPTER FOUR

IN THAT first week at the practice Giselle was made aware of a few things. One was that it left no time for moping, and another was that it might be a village surgery where she was working, but there was no hayseed atmosphere around the place.

Two part-time secretaries assisted the practice manager. All paperwork was dealt with by them. The receptionists were pleasant and efficient and the two practice nurses a pleasure to work with,

But why had she expected it to be any different? she asked herself. Marc might be bringing up two young children on his own, which was no easy task in anyone's book, and have sole responsibility for the surgery, but there was an air of competence about him that spoke of efficiency and it was there for all to see. They were a team and each one of them would go the extra mile for him if he asked them to.

When she'd arrived home after that first day her father had asked anxiously how it had gone. He'd sensed her reluctance to become involved in the community and though *he* was totally happy to be back where he came from, he knew that Giselle was not, and he was feeling that he'd been selfish in his demands on her.

'Not bad,' she'd told him. 'It seemed strange at first, but I've quite enjoyed it.'

He'd let out a sigh of relief. 'Thank goodness for that. If you'd said you hated it, I was going to suggest that you went back to Paris.'

'Paris? I couldn't do that,' she'd protested. 'Maybe one day, but not for some time yet. I want to see you fit and well before I even think of going back.

'So you're not pining for that fellow in the dress shop?'

'No. I'm not. It's over.' And she'd wondered

why it was Marc's face that had come to mind, instead of Raoul's.

Tom and Alice were now to be found in the fields at the back of the house when Giselle arrived home in the evenings, having been dropped off by their grandmother and left to play until Marc came to pick them up after the late surgery.

Her spirits always lifted when she saw them. It made her feel better to know that if the children weren't living in the house, at least they had the run of the land that it stood on.

But on the Friday afternoon at the end of that first week there was no sign of them, and Giselle felt disappointment tug at her. She'd started bringing them sweets from the village post office and they were usually on the lookout for her coming home each evening, but not this time.

When she went inside, the reason for their non-appearance was revealed. She found Alice sobbing in the kitchen, with Tom looking on uncomfortably and her father rummaging in the first-aid box.

'What's happened?' she asked.

'We were sitting on top of the gate, watching out for you,' Tom explained, 'and Alice fell off and bumped her head.'

'I'm looking for a plaster,' her father said.

'Let me examine her first,' Giselle told him. 'Her father will be along any moment. If we can calm Alice down and get it sorted out before he comes, it would be good.

'Don't cry, darling,' she told the little girl. 'I'm just going to look at where you bumped your head and then we'll see if we can stop it from hurting.'

There was a swelling on the side of Alice's head and it felt soft and spongy. 'Did Alice fall onto the grass or the concrete near the gate?' she asked Tom.

'She fell onto the concrete,' he replied.

Giselle nodded. She'd thought as much. The size of the swelling was proof of it.

"I'm going to bathe your head with something

nice and cool,' she told Alice, whose sobs were beginning to subside, 'and when your daddy comes we'll tell him all about it, shall we?'

Reaching into the first-aid box, she brought out a bottle of witch hazel and soaked a piece of boracic lint with it. She placed the lint on the swelling that seemed to be getting bigger by the minute and lifted Alice onto her knee for a comforting cuddle.

A ring on the front doorbell seconds later heralded Marc's arrival, and when her father went to let him in she heard him say, 'Giselle and the children are in the kitchen. Alice has had a fall and bumped her head.'

When Marc came striding in he caught his breath. His motherless daughter was sitting on Giselle's knee, sucking her thumb, with her tear-stained face up against her breasts and a wet piece of boracic lint flattened against the side of her head.

He would have expected her to throw herself into *his* safe arms, but surprisingly she didn't move, and when he asked what had happened Alice just cuddled closer to Giselle.

'They were sitting on the gate, waiting for me,' Giselle told him, 'and Alice fell off onto the concrete. I think we need to do something about the bump on her head.'

She'd said it casually enough, but her eyes had a message in them that was for him alone, and when he lifted up the dressing and felt the swelling, his expression was grave. But Marc was taking his cue from her and he said with equal calmness, 'Shall we have a ride to the hospital and let the doctor there make your head feel better, Alice?'

'No,' the little girl said.

'Not even if Giselle comes with us?'

Alice turned her head slowly and looked up questioningly into Giselle's face.

"Yes. I'll come, too, if you like,' Giselle said with a smile that concealed her anxiety.

'All right, then, Daddy,' Alice agreed with sudden drowsiness.

'Let's go,' he said and, with Giselle holding

Alice, he took Tom's hand and hurried them out to the car.

'Are you thinking what I'm thinking?' Marc asked grimly as they drove the short distance to the hospital.

'Haematoma?'

'Yes.'

'It could be. The swelling is soft and spongy to the touch. We'll be there in a moment, Marc, and then we'll know for certain.'

He was very pale and she thought achingly that this man had already lost his wife in an accident. How would he cope if anything happened to his daughter?

She looked down at Alice lying drowsily in the crook of her arm. Head injuries were tricky things. Only X-rays and a CT scan would show if there was any damage to the skull.

They rushed into A and E, and when the triage nurse saw Alice, now in her father's arms, she passed them straight through to the doctor on duty.

From then on it was action stations, with

Marc looking on with a ravaged expression as the necessary tests were done and Giselle keeping on the fringe of things with Tom. She was so glad to be there for them, but didn't want Marc to feel that she was intruding on his family crisis.

'Shall I ring your mother-in-law?' she asked.

'Yes, if you will,' he said. 'Margaret will be wondering where we've got to. Tom knows the number.'

'Oh, no!' Margaret Pollard exclaimed when Giselle explained what had happened. 'My poor lamb. Marc must be frantic.'

'Yes, he is,' Giselle told her.

'And who are you?' his mother-in-law asked. 'I didn't quite catch your name.'

'I'm Giselle Howard. I'm a doctor and Marc has asked me to work in the practice while your husband is ill.'

'Oh! I see,' she said, and Giselle knew that the woman at the other end of the line hadn't known about that. Maybe she'd been so busy looking after her sick husband and her grandchildren that she hadn't been tuned into the village grapevine, and maybe also she, Giselle, had been misleading herself by thinking that the rapport she felt with Marc was returned. It couldn't be if he hadn't thought fit to mention her to the only other woman in his life.

All the tests had been done and now they were waiting for the results. Alice was in a semi-doze, and Tom was taking in everything around him. His solemn blue gaze weighed up the equipment, the doctors and nurses going to and fro, and generally took in the hospital atmosphere while his father sat holding Alice's small hand.

Giselle wanted to go to his side and comfort him. Hold him close like she'd held his daughter, but she didn't know him well enough for that. He had withdrawn into a sombre shell of his own and she doubted if he even remembered she was there. Until he looked up suddenly and as their glances held he said, 'Thanks for being here with us, Giselle.'

'I wouldn't want to be anywhere else,' she

told him. 'I'll do anything you want of me if it will help.'

At that moment there was a footstep on the tiled corridor outside the cubicle where they were waiting and the consultant who'd seen them earlier appeared. He was smiling. 'Do you want the good news or the good news?' he asked.

Neither of them answered, but in each hope was surfacing.

'No bleeding. No skull fractures,' he told them briefly. 'You were wise to bring Alice to us, but fortunately the softness of the swollen area where she bumped her head was nothing more than the reaction from a child's soft tissue. There will be some soreness and bruising for a while and that should be all. If you have any further worries, bring her back to us straight away, but I would expect her to be fine in a day or two.'

Marc's face was slack with relief, but it didn't stop him from asking, 'What about the drowsiness, though?'

'You and your wife,' he said, with his glance

on Giselle, 'know your daughter better than anyone. But I would think it is due to either reaction from the fall, exhaustion from crying or maybe it is just because it's her bedtime. However, as I've just said, if you have any concerns, we are always here.'

Giselle had felt her colour rise when the consultant had mistaken her for Alice's mother, but as they drove back to the village Marc had no comment to make. He merely remarked that he'd suddenly realised he was starving and that she must be, too.

'I wasn't before,' she told him, 'but I'm hungry now. It is surprising how one's appetite disappears in times of crisis.'

He nodded. 'Margaret will have had a meal waiting for me. What did she say when you rang?'

'She was shocked, upset and wondered who I was and what I was doing at the hospital with you, until I explained.'

'Mmm. She *would* be upset.' he said, and didn't comment further.

When they stopped outside Abbeyfields Alice was awake and she said, 'I promise I won't sit on the gate anymore, Giselle.'

'That's good news, Alice,' she said softly. 'Your daddy was very worried about the bump on your head.'

'Were *you* worried?' the little girl wanted to know.

'Yes, I was,' Giselle told her gravely. 'Especially when I came home and you weren't in the fields. But I think your daddy wants to get you both tucked up in bed, so I'll say goodbye, and if I don't see you tomorrow I'll know it's because he wants you to rest until your head is better.'

When she looked at Marc he was shaking his head as if that was going to be easier said than done. Then he was making his own farewell, telling her, 'I'll see you on Monday, Giselle.'

'Why not let me take the Saturday morning surgery?' she suggested. 'You've had a worrying experience and look as if you could do with some rest yourself, *and* you wouldn't have to take the children round to your in-laws'.'

'Do you feel you could cope?' he asked, his expression lightening. 'I could bring Craig in to assist you.'

'I can manage on my own,' she assured him, not relishing being alone with the young doctor who had made it quite obvious he'd like to get to know her a lot better. 'The receptionist will help me out if I get stuck with anything.'

'All right, offer accepted,' Marc said, smiling for the first time since he'd arrived at Abbeyfields and found Alice in tears with a bump on her head. 'I might even manage a lie-in if the children don't wake too early.' And with a wave for her father, who was watching them anxiously from the open front door, he drove off.

'Having seen that Alice was with you, am I to take it that there was no serious injury?' Philip asked once she was inside.

'Yes, thank goodness,' she told him. 'Both

Marc and I were very concerned, but the tests they did at the hospital showed that there were no serious injuries to Alice's head.'

'Yes, well, better safe than sorry. I felt for him when he came in and saw what had happened.'

'Marc lost his wife in an accident,' she explained. 'So you can imagine what was going through his mind.'

'Did he, now? And how would you know that?'

'Because he told me. That's how. It was embarrassing at the hospital. The consultant thought I was Alice's mother.'

'Did he, now?' her father repeated.

On the point of putting a ready meal into the microwave, Giselle said. 'Will you please stop saying that, *papa?*'

'All right,' he agreed equably. 'But unless you're game for it, watch out. If the good doctor hasn't got you mapped out as a ready-made mother, it seemed to me that little girl certainly has.'

'Nonsense!' she said snappily. 'Anyway, I

would have to be out of my mind to consider anything like that.'

But later, standing alone in the moonlight beside the infamous gate, Giselle was remembering how small and vulnerable Alice had felt in her arms and her heart ached for the two motherless children.

It was Marc who had caught her imagination in the first place, but it now felt as if all three of them were gradually invading the privacy that she was trying to hang on to. Don't let them, she told herself. You didn't cross the Channel to become a ready-made mother for anyone.

In his sprawling semi-detached at the other side of the village Marc was seated in his neglected garden, thinking *his* thoughts. The children were fast asleep and now he was looking back sombrely on the events of the afternoon and evening.

He was thankful that Alice was asleep in her own bed instead of being in hospital, and with the memory of those few fraught hours came a vision of the way she'd cuddled up to Giselle and had wanted her to go with them to the hospital.

He wondered what the reluctant GP with her toned-down elegance had thought about it all. He felt as if he'd been crowding her ever since she'd arrived in the village and now he had involved her with his children, too.

When the consultant at the hospital had thought Giselle was his wife, he had averted his glance instead of explaining that she was just a friend. He knew that she did not like being discussed and had felt that the less said,the less embarrassment on both their parts, but it hadn't stopped him from wishing, though he wasn't sure what for.

Alice hadn't been the only one grateful for Giselle's presence. It had been good that for once he'd had another adult with him in a crisis. He was calm and capable in most things, but when it came to his children he was no different from any other anxious parent.

As the moon replaced the sun in a summer

sky he got out of the garden chair and stretched wearily. The chances of him getting a lie-in in the morning were pretty remote, he thought wryly, but there was nothing to stop him from having an early night.

After checking that Alice was sleeping peacefully and straightening the covers over Tom, he went into his own room, ready to sleep the night away, but it was not to be. At any other time he would have been out like a light the moment his head touched the pillow, yet not tonight, and eventually, after tossing and turning for what seemed like hours, he got out of bed and padded across to the window.

He could see the chimneys of Abbeyfields rising starkly in the distance in the moon's light and knew that the reason for his restlessness was there, inside the old house. He wanted Giselle as he had never wanted any other woman in the whole of his life.

It was as if she'd been sent to him. But sent for what? Not to fall into his arms, panting with desire, he thought bleakly. It was more a case of her being sent to remind him of what was lacking in his life.

Before meeting her, he'd been contented enough in a blunted sort of way, and had occasionally thought that he might marry again one day, to someone local perhaps. But there'd been no urgency in him, as no woman he'd come across had ever got through to him to the extent that he'd been ready to take a second chance.

Now he knew why. He had been waiting for Giselle, and now that she was here, was he going to do something about it and risk making a fool of himself or did he let it lie and spend the rest of his days yearning?

She had surprised him by offering to take the Saturday morning surgery and he'd felt it was a step in the right direction, but that was connected with their working lives, and business was the last thing in his mind at that moment. He was filled with dawning wonder and a glum certainty that if she knew how he felt, the barriers would go up.

* * *

When Giselle arrived at the surgery the next morning, Mollie was on duty in Reception and she smiled when she saw her.

'Are you standing in to give Dr Bannerman a break after last night's trauma?' she asked.

'Something like that,' Giselle told her, thinking that the bush telegraph was working well.

'Alice *is* all right, isn't she?' Mollie asked.

'Yes. A scan and X-rays showed that all was well.'

'Thank goodness. Her father has had enough to cope with, losing her mother like he did.'

'Yes, that must have been very sad,' Giselle murmured, not sure if she wanted to hear any more about Marc's personal life, but it looked as if she was going to have to.

'That one was never in,' Mollie said scathingly. 'Always galloping around the place on that horse of hers, preening herself. You'd have thought she was training for the equestrian team in the Olympics.

'Amanda's parents, Margaret and Stanley,

are well respected hereabouts and they've been there every step of the way for Dr Bannerman and the children.'

At that moment the door opened and the first patient came into the waiting room. Grasping the opportunity to get away from Mollie's gossip, Giselle went to her desk and began to read through his notes.

There were not many of them and none were recent, so it seemed that the patient was normally a healthy person, and when Trevor Kershaw seated himself opposite her, that was easy to believe. Of trim build with clear eyes and a fresh complexion, he immediately gave the impression of an outdoors type of person, and when he began to explain why he was there, it seemed that was the case.

'I'm gamekeeper to a landowner who owns a big place on the tops,' he said, 'and a couple of weeks ago I got shot.'

'Shot!' Giselle echoed.

He smiled a mirthless smile. 'Yes.'

'I see.'

'It was an accident. Being a stranger to the place, you may not know that we start shooting grouse up on the moors on the twelfth of August, and my boss always invites some of his city friends to join in the shoot. I discovered that not all of them have a straight aim,' he went on dryly, 'and I got hit in the leg.'

'Mmm. It sounds a rather dangerous pastime.'

'Not if people know what they're doing. Anyhow, I went to A and E. They got the pellets out of my leg and I thought that was the end of it, but I'm getting a lot of pain from the place where they went in, and I'm wondering if I should go back to the hospital or persevere and see if it goes.'

'Let me see where you were hit,' she said, and he pushed down the thick sock that he was wearing over corduroy trousers. Lifting his trouser leg, he displayed the calf, which was still showing the marks of his ordeal.

'Your leg looks healthy enough,' Giselle said after she had examined it. 'There are no signs of infection, so I don't think that any of the pellets are still in there, but the impact could have damaged the muscle. You may need physiotherapy to relieve the pain. But first you need to have it X-rayed again. I wouldn't imagine there would be any splintering of the bone as the pellets entered a fleshy part of your leg, and they would have checked for that when you went to the hospital, but you do need to go back and let them have another look. Also, wearing the thick sock over your trousers could be restricting the circulation around the affected area. Try wearing shorts for a day or two. But do go back to A and E, just to be on the safe side.'

As he was leaving, she heard Marc's voice in Reception and when she went to investigate he was chatting to Mollie, the children by his side.

'I thought you were supposed to be having a rest,' she said, and with her glance switching to Alice, who was beaming across at her, she said, 'And how are you this morning, Alice? Has the bump gone down?'

She could see that it had. There was no need

to ask, though there was still a lot of bruising, but she felt that the little girl wouldn't want the previous day's catastrophe to be dismissed too lightly.

Marc hadn't spoken so far. Giselle wasn't to know it, but he was momentarily speechless. In the dark hours of the night he had admitted to himself that he was already in love with the slender, brown haired doctor standing in front of him, and it was taking all his control not to take her in his arms and tell her how he felt.

But it was Tom's turn to have something to say, almost as if he felt that it was time that *he* had some attention.

'I want to be a doctor when I grow up,' he announced. 'I liked it at the hospital last night. All those machines and the doctors in their white coats, and I won't be bothered about all the blood.'

Marc was recovering from those first few moments of seeing Giselle again and he said, 'Good. We'll have to see if you still feel the same when you've done your A Levels.'

'I won't change my mind,' Tom told his father. 'I've seen what they do on TV.'

'I don't want to be a nurse,' Alice piped up. 'I want to be a ballerina.'

Giselle was smiling, and Marc said quizzically, 'So that's their careers settled…from the wards to the arts.' Then, on a more serious note, he asked, 'How's it going, Giselle?'

'Fine,' she told him. 'I've only seen one patient so far. A man called Trevor Kershaw, who is recovering from a gunshot wound.'

'Ah! Was it an accident?'

'Yes.'

'He's gamekeeper on one of the big estates. What happened?'

'He said they were grouse shooting and he got hit.'

He nodded. 'You won't be familiar with our rural customs, but that's what they do at this time of year. You remember Frank, the man with the artificial leg? Well, his son, Toby, is a beater. A lot of the locals make extra cash by doing that at this time of the year. Their job is to beat the grass to make the birds rise into the air where they can be seen.'

'It sounds cruel and dangerous.'

'I suppose it is,' he agreed.

Alice was pulling at his sleeve.

'Can we go and play in Giselle's fields?' she wanted to know.

Marc shook his head.

'Not today, Alice. After that nasty bump I want to keep my eye on you. How would you like to go for a picnic this afternoon?'

'Ye-es!' both children chorused, and he glanced across at Giselle.

'I don't suppose you'd like to join us? I'll ask Jenny at the baker's to make us a picnic basket. She does it for the walkers and anyone else requiring sustenance.'

Giselle could feel her colour rising. She was tempted to say yes, but her thoughts of the night before came crowding back. The small family waiting for her reply would be so easy to love, and that was not on her agenda. She was being drawn into their lives and she wanted to go back to Paris one day. She didn't want to start putting down roots in this place, but neither did she want to hurt Marc and his children.

He was watching her expression and wishing he hadn't said anything. It had been on impulse because he was so desperate to be with her, and he knew instinctively that she was going to refuse.

'It's OK,' he said easily, as if he wasn't bothered either way. 'If you've something else planned, it's fine.'

'Yes. I have, actually,' she told him, knowing it to be a lie, and when tears of disappointment began to run down Alice's face, she wanted to change her mind. But Marc was comforting his daughter and telling her gently, 'I'm sure that Giselle will come with us another time.'

'Yes, of course I will,' she said uncomfortably, and as patient number two appeared on the horizon Marc said, 'We'll be off, then. Have a nice weekend, Giselle.'

There wasn't much hope of that, she thought

when they'd gone. Alice had cried when she'd lied to them and she'd wanted to sweep her up into her arms, kiss away her tears and tell her that she'd changed her mind, but she hadn't done so and now the weekend stretched ahead like a barren desert.

On Sunday night she decided that she'd done enough moping around the house. She was going to see Marc and explain why she'd refused his invitation.

When he answered the door to her, his face went blank with surprise. Then he stepped back and said, 'Come in. Is anything wrong?'

Giselle shook her head.

'No, not really,' she told him. 'I just felt that I owed you an explanation.'

'Regarding what?' Before she could reply, he went on, 'Do you mind coming through to the kitchen? I'm doing the weekly ironing.'

She smiled. 'No, I don't mind at all. I'll give you a hand if you like.'

'No need,' he told her abruptly. 'I can manage.'

'I didn't say you couldn't,' she told him

mildly, with a feeling that she'd chosen the wrong moment.

'I was just about to stop for a coffee. Would you like to join me before you tell me why you've come? We won't be interrupted. The children are asleep.'

She didn't want a coffee. Didn't want anything except the opportunity to clear the air, but he had asked and it would seem churlish to refuse, so she said, 'Yes, I'd love a coffee and while you're making it, I'll help out with the ironing.'

'Shall we take it into the garden?' Marc said, once he'd presented her with the steaming brew.

'Yes, wherever,' she agreed, and followed him outside.

There was silence between them as they drank the coffee, but the moment she put the cup down Marc said, 'Fire away.'

'There isn't all that much to say,' she told him, 'except that I feel I should explain why I didn't accept the offer to picnic with you and the children.'

'Hold it right there, Giselle,' he interrupted. 'You don't have to explain yourself to me about *anything*. You're a free spirit and want to remain so, and I don't blame you. We've been crowding you and I'm sorry.'

'It isn't like that at all,' she protested. 'You have nothing to be sorry about, Marc. You've done more to lift me out of the doldrums since I came here than anyone. It's just that I hope to go back to Paris one day and I wouldn't want the children to get too attached to me and then be upset when I leave.'

'So we haven't charmed you enough to make you want to stay, then?'

'It isn't a case of that, and if I do go back it won't be until I'm sure that my father will be all right without me. You do understand, don't you?' she pleaded. 'It's just that I've lived there all my life, just as you have lived here all your life, and I'm sure that you wouldn't want to leave this place to go and live in Paris.'

He was tempted to tell her that he would go and live at the North Pole if she asked him to, but it was there in her eyes, the need to know that he understood, and he thought dismally that the annoying thing was that he did. He understood only too well.

Giselle was young and very beautiful and he was a widower with two children that he loved too much to think of uprooting them. But that was a decision he wasn't going to have to make, as she'd just made it clear that she was merely passing through. Passing through the village and passing through his life.

'So do you want the children to stop playing in your fields?' he asked levelly.

'No, of course not!' Giselle exclaimed. 'It's lovely to see them there.'

'You don't mind having *some* contact with them, then?'

'I don't mind at all, and will you, please, stop making me sound like someone who doesn't like children? I'm merely trying to explain how my life is mapped out.'

She didn't say, 'and it doesn't include *you*

long term,' but he'd like to bet that was what she was thinking.

But Marc was wrong. As their glances held, Giselle was deciding that it would be so easy to love this big blond man. For a short time in the past she'd imagined Raoul waiting for her in a smart morning suit as she floated down the aisle in one of his filmy creations. But that had been before she'd discovered that the only person *he* loved was himself. In stark contrast to this village doctor, who had time to spare for everyone, including herself.

Marc sighed. 'If you want to keep a low profile with the children, fine, but I'm afraid that you're lumbered with me, as we'll be together all the time at the practice.'

He was making her feel bad, she thought. It was clear from his manner that she'd upset him. She certainly hadn't meant to, but he couldn't be expected to know that she was already attracted to him and panicking at the thought.

She got to her feet. 'I'm going, Marc. I should never have come.'

He had risen also and as he faced her amongst the shrubs and summer flowers he said, 'Is it this that you're afraid of, Giselle?' He leaned forward and kissed her gently on the mouth, and as she stiffened in surprise he murmured against her lips, 'Or this?'

He kissed her again and this time it wasn't gentle. It was demanding, searching, warming her blood, making her heart race, so much so that when it was over and his arms fell away she almost lost her balance.

'I'm sorry,' he groaned as he reached out to steady her. 'I've just made matters worse, haven't I?'

Giselle didn't answer. She picked up the jacket that she'd taken off while ironing, opened the front door and walked out into the night.

CHAPTER FIVE

WHEN Giselle arrived back at Abbeyfields, her father had gone to bed and she had the sitting room to herself. Kicking off her shoes, she flung herself onto the sofa and lay looking blindly up at the ceiling.

Why had he done it? she asked herself. She'd just explained that she wouldn't be staying any longer than she had to, and he seemed to have got the message that she didn't want to put down any roots. Then, on the very moment of her leaving, he had wiped out the sensible conversation they'd just had by kissing her... And it had been some kiss!

Had he done it to test her reaction? To make a point? Show her that this place *did* have something to offer—*him*? Yet she knew that

Marc didn't see himself in that light. There was no conceit in him.

Though how could *she* possibly know what was in his mind? She'd only known him for a short time. Maybe he had used his sexuality, and he had plenty of that, to make her change her mind to suit his own ends. He needed her at the surgery, for one thing. But it wasn't as if she was the only doctor available, and *would* he go to such lengths?

Anger was surfacing inside her now. She could lie there forever, trying to work it out, and she would be no wiser. From now on she would keep Marc at a distance, she decided.

The sensible thing to do would be to leave the practice, but much to her surprise she was enjoying being part of the small team who looked after the health of the villagers. Why should she let him drive her away? His words came back to haunt her. 'I'm afraid you're lumbered with me,' he'd said. At the time she'd thought nothing of it, but now she wondered what he'd meant.

Giselle went up the stairs to bed with the annoyance still in her, but the moment she lay down to sleep it faded and all she could think of were those moments in his arms. Raoul had never kissed her like that. She didn't think he would know how. Marc had made her feel cherished and desirable, and she'd been short on cherishing of late.

She'd had a warm and loving relationship with her mother and missed her dreadfully, but that had been the love of mother and daughter. When Marc had held her in his arms it had been the attraction of the sexes, something else that was missing, and she'd never expected to find it in this small village beneath the peaks. But maybe she was making too much of it. She was not going to let one kiss throw her off course.

She turned her face into the pillow, deciding that she could go on all night thinking this, thinking that, still ending up confused, and at last she drifted into a restless sleep.

* * *

Marc made no attempt to follow Giselle when she left. He was overcome by what he saw as his complete stupidity. Giselle had been a visitor in his house and he had come on to her like a sex-starved maniac. What had happened to the sensible widower who had decided to be cautious in his approach to the woman he'd fallen in love with? She'd only just told him that she wouldn't be staying in the village, that she was going back to France at the first opportunity. And the next moment he'd been kissing her, willing her to feel the same as he did.

He wouldn't be surprised if Giselle didn't turn up in the morning, and if she didn't he would have only himself to blame. He was in love, really in love for the first time in his life. From the moment she'd arrived the previous night he'd been so aware of her it wasn't surprising that for an enchanted moment he'd forgotten that he'd intended to play it cool.

* * *

Marc was the last to arrive again at the surgery the next morning, due to being awake most of the night and then over-sleeping. Breakfast had been a rushed affair and by the time he'd dropped the children off at school he'd been running late.

Reception was empty when he got there, but the waiting room was full and he caught a glimpse of a patient going into Craig's room. The door next to it was shut and his heart sank. It was as he'd expected. After last night Giselle had decided to call it a day.

It opened suddenly and she was there, bidding her first patient of the morning goodbye and about to call in the next one.

'We need to talk,' he said in a low voice.

She shook her head. 'No, we don't. I discovered last night that talking is wasted on you.'

'Let me explain.'

'There is nothing to explain. Just let me get on with the job if you don't mind.' She was smiling, but not at him. It was directed at someone behind him. 'Come in, Mrs Pritchard,' she said, 'and tell me what I can do for you.'

The local hairdresser gave a wry smile, 'You can tell me if I've got carpal tunnel syndrome, Doctor.' And as Giselle went into her room and closed the door behind her, Marc went to start the day without his usual calm composure.

Joan Pritchard had worked in her hairdresser's shop in the village for more than thirty years and the job that was all hand and arm movement was beginning to take its toll.

'What makes you think you might have carpal tunnel syndrome?' Giselle asked as she examined Joan's hands.

'I know of another hairdresser who has it and I've got the same symptoms,' the patient explained.

'And what are they?'

'Numbness, tingling and pain in my fingers and thumb that's often worse at night.'

'Those *are* the symptoms,' Giselle agreed. 'It's caused by sustained pressure on the median nerve where it passes through a gap called the carpal tunnel under a ligament at the front of the wrist.

'I'm going to make you an hospital appointment so that a diagnosis can be made by measuring the number of impulses going through the median nerve to the wrist. If the problem is what it appears to be, they might think it necessary for you to sleep with your hand in a splint. Or a small amount of a corticosteroid drug injected beneath the ligament could solve the problem. The good news is that this kind of thing often disappears of its own accord.'

The hairdresser's expression brightened. 'That would indeed be a bonus. I'm a widow with two teenage children. My business is my livelihood. I can't afford to shut up shop.'

'So let's get it sorted out,' Giselle told her. 'If the problem is what we think, it is treatable. That's the main thing.'

Joan nodded. 'I know I haven't come with a complaint that applies only to women, but if ever that does happen, it will be good to have a woman doctor treating me. I hope that you'll be with us for a long time to come, Dr Howard.'

When surgery was over, Giselle was writing up the last patient's notes when Marc came in. She observed him warily and he said abruptly, 'I'm here on business—not pleasure.

'The results have come through on Frank Fairbank's scan and the lump in his groin *is* cancer. I'm going up to the farm to see him now, and I'd like you to come with me on the home visits as usual.'

Giselle got to her feet.

'If you say so.'

'I do…and in case you have any doubts, I promise not to ravish you in a lay-by.'

Her colour was rising.

'I'm glad you think what happened last night is funny. For myself, I just can't see the joke.'

Neither could he, Marc thought miserably, so why was he making matters worse? Just the mere sight of her was making his loins ache. But after last night the chances of Giselle ever feeling the same about him were extremely low.

On the drive up to the farm on the moors they were both silent. Giselle's glance was on the capable hands on the steering-wheel and the unreadable profile of the man who was never out of her thoughts. If only her father had been happy to stay in Paris, none of this would have happened, she thought. She wouldn't be torn two ways between the place she loved and this stranger who held the reins of family and health care so firmly in his hands.

The gateposts of the farm were looming up ahead and the familiar sick feeling that came with the giving of bad news to a patient was there. It was like the last time. Toby came round from the back of the farm buildings when he heard the car pull up, and the anxious question they'd seen so many times before was there in his eyes.

'It's bad news, isn't it?' he said. 'I can tell from your faces.'

Marc laid a comforting hand on Toby's arm. 'Where's your Dad, Toby?' he asked.

'In bed. He's not feeling too good this

morning. Go on up. I'll take my boots off, wash my hands and be right with you.'

When they went inside, Giselle saw that there was clutter everywhere. If ever she'd seen a house that lacked a woman's touch, this was it.

The first thing on view when they went into the bedroom was Frank's artificial leg on a chair beside the bed, and she wondered how much use that would be to him if he had to have surgery in the groin.

He raised himself up on the pillows and a pair of bright eyes looked them over.

'I know what you're going to say, Marc,' he said, before Marc could speak. 'I've got the dreaded lurgy, haven't I? They said as much when I was at the hospital.'

'It's a sarcoma, Frank,' Marc told him gently. 'That's the bad news. The good news is that it hasn't spread.'

'What's a sarcoma?' Toby's voice said from the doorway.

'In this case it's cancer in the tissue. Not in the bone or in an organ.'

'And does that give Dad a better chance?' his son asked.

'Yes, if it hasn't spread. They will operate to remove it and then either suggest radiotherapy or chemotherapy.'

The sick man laughed hollowly. 'I don't think I want to be bothered.'

'Don't talk like that, Dad,' his son begged.

'Toby's right, Frank,' Marc told him. 'I've never seen anyone as brave as you were when your leg was trapped beneath the tractor. Nothing could be worse than that.'

'Aye, maybe,' the old farmer said dryly, 'but I was younger then…and tougher.'

'When is your appointment with the oncologist?'

'Next week.'

'So you've got time to think about it…and while you're doing that, consider what it will be like for Toby if you decide to give up on life.'

'All right. I'll think about it,' Frank agreed, 'but if there's one place where I don't want anybody meddling, it's where my false leg fits, and that's exactly what they'll be doing.'

When they went downstairs Toby said, 'Just look at this place. I never seem to have the time to tidy it up, with the farm to look after and Dad not being well.'

Giselle spoke for the first time. 'You should be entitled to a carer and some help with cleaning under the circumstances. Leave it with us, and we'll see what we can do.'

Toby smiled gratefully. 'That would be good. Just to find a clean cup would be heaven.'

'Poor guys,' Marc said sombrely as they drove back down the hill road. 'If I know Frank, his decision will be based on what he thinks will be best for Toby, but whatever he decides life won't be easy for them over the coming weeks. The more help we can get them, the better.'

He looked across at Giselle and saw a tear roll down her cheek. 'What's wrong?' he asked anxiously as he pulled in at the side of the road.

'Just memories, that's all. *Maman* died from cancer. She was beautiful, kind and loving.

My father and I were devastated when we lost her. That's why he couldn't bear to stay where they'd been so happy and came back here. It was the last thing I wanted for myself, but he was exhausted and lonely without her. The least I could do was fall in with his wishes.'

Marc longed to take her into his arms and comfort her, but Giselle might think it was going to be a repeat of the previous night. If he had to tread carefully for ever, he wasn't going to risk upsetting her again.

'What you've just told me explains more clearly why you are so unhappy here,' he said soberly. 'If I didn't understand just how much, I'm sorry.'

'I'm not so much unhappy as out of my natural habitat,' she told him, wiping away the tears. 'Some people can adjust to any kind of surroundings. Maybe I'm not one of them. But there is one thing you should know, just in case you think all I can do is criticise. I have had my eyes opened with regard to the way you run your country practice and feel honoured to be part of it.'

He was smiling. 'So I'm not entirely out of favour.'

She was forgiving him already, Giselle was thinking. So much for her vow to be cool and distant with him. But how could she stay angry with this loving father and compassionate doctor? One day he would marry again and she hoped that whoever he chose would be kind to him and his beautiful children.

With Tom and Alice in mind, she asked, 'How is the bump? Has the bruising disappeared?'

'More or less,' he told her, taking his glance off the mouth that had tempted him so much the night before. It was incredible how Giselle affected him. Since Amanda's death his sex life had been nonexistent, and it hadn't been anything to boast about before that, as her restlessness had made them like ships that passed in the night.

But since meeting Giselle, the longing to make love to her was like a gnawing ache inside him, and that was how it was going to have to stay. She'd made it clear that she had no interest in him except as her employer and had also been emphatic that returning to Paris one day was still the uppermost thought in her mind.

As they pulled up in front of the practice they caught a glimpse of the back view of Irene Jackson going inside. Marc groaned.

'It looks as if Irene is back with us.' he said. 'It would seem that the hospital wasn't prepared to dance to her tune. They've written to me to confirm that it is Munchausen's syndrome that Irene is suffering from and say that she was very disruptive when they found nothing wrong with her.'

'I'll see her if you like,' Giselle volunteered.

He smiled across at her. 'I wouldn't wish that on you.'

'Let me.'

'Well, all right, if you insist, but be warned. You'll be in for a long session.'

'Nobody believes me when I say I'm sick,'

was Irene's opening comment, and Giselle thought that the poor woman was trapped in her own fantasies. She wasn't wrong when she said she was sick, but it was a sickness of the mind rather than the body, and how did she explain to her?

'I believe you when you say you are sick,' she told her gently. 'You *have* got an illness, and it is something very rare.'

The disturbed patient was observing her expectantly, calm for once as she waited to hear what was coming next.

'It is called Munchausen's syndrome.'

'I knew I wasn't wrong!' Irene cried triumphantly. 'I just knew it.'

'You are wrong in one way,' Giselle told her patiently. 'You're *not* ill, but you have an illness that makes you think you are. Does that make sense?'

'No. It doesn't,' the woman said flatly. 'I don't know what you mean.'

'It *is* difficult to understand, I agree. But the next time that someone tells you that you aren't ill, explain that you have Munchausen's syndrome, and if they know anything about health care, they will understand.'

Irene departed on that note and Giselle wondered just how much she'd understood of what she'd said, but at least she was finding some contentment in the knowledge that she *did* have an illness.

'That was quick,' Marc said when she'd gone. 'Irene actually looked happy as she was leaving.'

'I tried a little homespun psychology by explaining that she *did* have an illness and it was the kind that made her think she had other illnesses. I don't know how much she understood but she went home content. For how long is another matter.'

He was smiling.

'Well done. I can see that you are clever as well as beautiful.'

She turned away. It was hard not to respond to his teasing flattery, but the truth of it was that she'd never felt less beautiful in her life. She went through the motions and was immaculate when she turned up at the surgery each day, but there was no joy in it.

Life after a bereavement was a matter of getting through the days until the pain gradually eased. That and the hurt from being so casually dismissed by Raoul when she'd desperately needed a shoulder to cry on were two of the reasons why looking in the mirror had become a formality rather than a pleasure.

When they were due to leave at the end of the day Marc said, 'Tom and Alice won't be round at your place when you get home, Giselle. She seems all right after Friday night's panic, but I felt another day taking it calmly would do her no harm. I've asked my mother-in-law to make sure she doesn't do anything too exhausting. If it's all right with you, they'll be round tomorrow, or would you rather they didn't come?'

She knew immediately what he meant. Marc was remembering what she'd said the night before about not getting too close. But Tom and Alice romping around the fields was a different thing to them all picnicking together. Surely he could see that.

'Of course not. We love to see them playing out there away from the traffic. Dad can see them from the house and keeps an eye on them. It's something for them to do while they're off school for the summer holidays *and* it gives their grandparents a break.'

He held up a placatory hand. 'All right. That's fine, then. It's just that I thought I ought to clarify the situation.'

He'd done it again, she thought as she drove the short distance to Abbeyfields—made her feel uncharitable. Apart from his in-laws, who had their own problems at the moment, Marc coped with the children single-handedly and he must think her mean if he had to ask if she still wanted Tom and Alice to come round to play.

When she arrived home the following night her heart lifted at the sight of them roaming free as they'd done before Alice had fallen off the gate.

Her father's thoughts must have been running along the same lines, as when she appeared he said, 'It's good to have the children back with us, isn't it, and to know that Alice is over that nasty tumble. Their grandma brought them round as usual. I made her a cup of tea and we had a nice chat. You haven't met her, have you?'

'Er, no.'

'I know her from the old days. When she brought them round that first time I recognised her as another face from the past. We used to play tennis together, Jenny from the bakery, James, who has the garden centre, Margaret and myself. We've played many a doubles match on the tennis courts in the park. She was surprised when she discovered that it was me who had bought Abbeyfields. I would have thought that news travels fast in these parts, but it seems not.'

'It does usually,' she assured him, 'but the Pollards will have been too concerned with Dr Pollard's illness to be interested in village gossip. He has had a bad dose of shingles and is still not at all well.'

'I suppose you could be right,' he agreed. 'One thing is for sure, Marc hasn't said much to them about *you.*'

That was not surprising, Giselle thought. He'd been married to their daughter and even though he was free, he would be careful what he said about the opposite sex. The Pollards would be aware that one day he might find himself a new wife, who would share in the upbringing of Alice and Tom, and it must be a worrying thought. Their daughter's children in the care of another woman.

Tom had appeared at the kitchen door, with Alice close behind. He was waving a piece of paper. 'It's for you, Giselle,' he said.

'For me!' she exclaimed.

It was a drawing of herself and she had to hide a smile. He was watching her expectantly and she knew that for Tom, the more reserved of the two children, it was a special gesture. A matchstick woman with long brown hair that looked like rat's tails and a very wide mouth was looking up at her.

'Do you like it?' he asked with an anxious frown, and she wanted to bend down and kiss his furrowed brow. Instead she told him, 'It's amazing, Tom. You even remembered what I was wearing the last time we met.' Sure enough, he'd drawn the navy suit and lime green top that she'd had on when they'd called at the surgery on the previous Saturday morning.

Not to be outdone, Alice thrust a handful of tiny white daisies at her, saying, 'I've gathered these for you, Giselle.'

'How lovely!' she exclaimed, as a lump came up in her throat. 'Do you know how to make a daisy chain?'

Alice shook her head.

'Come and sit by me and I'll show you,' she said.

When Marc arrived to take them home he found the drawing propped up on the bookcase in pride of place and Giselle and Alice painstakingly finishing the daisy chain.'

While Tom's attention was on the glass of juice that her father was pouring for him, Marc was admiring the drawing and he said in a low voice that was for her ears alone, 'It would seem that beauty is in the eye of the beholder.'

'It's lovely,' she said. 'I shall keep it always.'

'Will you?' he asked, serious now. 'Will it be something to remember us by?'

'That, and other things.'

'What other things?'

'*You,* and what you are. But don't badger me, Marc.' Looking down at Alice, who was engrossed in what they were doing, she changed the subject.

'My father knows your mother-in-law from way back. They used to play tennis together.'

'Really?' he commented absently, his mind on the feeling of togetherness in the room. There was the beautiful Parisian with her smooth golden skin and high cheekbones, beneath the amazing eyes that Tom had drawn as two blobs. The old man fussing over the boy, and Alice in another world with her daisy chain. His children, happy and content because they were fitting Giselle into the empty place in their lives. Giselle, who had other ideas, other plans that weren't going to include any of them.

'Tom, Alice, we need to be off,' he said abruptly. 'Grandma will be waiting for us.' As they opened their mouths simultaneously to protest he said, 'No arguing. If you've left anything in the fields, go and get it.'

'Thanks for having them again,' he told Giselle and her father in the same abrupt tone, and as she eyed him questioningly she had no idea that now it was his turn to be concerned in case the children became too fond of her.

They were still coming to play each day, but since Tuesday Giselle had made sure that they were not inside the house when Marc came to pick them up. He'd been his usual good-humoured self the following morning, but it hadn't stopped her from thinking that it was something to do with the scene he'd walked in on that had upset him.

She'd been on to Social Services to get some help for Frank and Toby, and when she'd met the younger of the two men one lunchtime in Jenny's baker's shop, he'd said, 'They've found us a home help, Dr Howard. I don't know why we didn't do something about it sooner. We're having to pay, but we don't mind that. I'd almost forgotten what home comforts were. She's a homely body and Dad gets on with her a treat.'

Giselle had been pleased to see him in such good spirits, but his expression had sobered when she'd asked if his father had decided what he was going to do about surgery.

'He just grunts every time I ask him,' Toby had said. 'He sees the oncologist next Tuesday so that will be decision time.'

'Shall I ask Dr Bannerman to call to have another word with him?' she'd suggested.

'You can if you like, but I don't think it will

do much good. My dad is a stubborn old guy. Once he makes his mind up, nothing will shift him.'

On the Friday night of that same week, Giselle went home feeling that it seemed like a lifetime since they'd gone rushing to hospital with Alice. Since then there had been happier moments, like Tom presenting her with the drawing, but standing out above the rest had been that kiss.

She wished she could forget it. It wasn't as if she'd never been kissed before, far from it. There had been passionate moments with Raoul, but she'd never slept with him and had wondered if that was the reason why he'd been so quick to dump her.

With Marc it had been different from anything she'd ever known before. For one thing, it had been totally unexpected, just as she'd finished explaining that she wanted no involvement in village life. Yet she'd responded as if their previous discussion had never taken place. Until reason had triumphed and she'd fled.

In the working side of her life the most memorable events of the week had been the upsetting news they'd had to convey to Frank Fairbank and the time spent with Irene, who so desperately wanted to be ill...and wasn't.

She was settling in, she thought. Against all her resolves she was starting to care about the village and its people, and top of the list were a small girl and boy and their father.

CHAPTER SIX

To THE relief of all concerned, Frank Fairbank decided to have the operation.

'It took just a few words from Mary, the home help, to convince him that he had to go ahead with it,' Toby told Marc incredulously when he called in at the surgery the following week. 'He's only known her a matter of days, while I've been talking myself blue in the face to get him to have the operation.'

Marc smiled. 'And what did this amazing woman say that did the trick?'

'She teases him all the time,' Toby said. 'When he told her his concerns about not being able to wear Arty any more—that's the name she's given his false leg—she told him that he would be just as fanciable on crutches and to stop crossing his bridges before he got to them.'

'How old is Mary?' Marc asked.

'In her sixties, I'd say. She has a daughter about my age who's been round a couple of times to give her a lift.'

'Are they local?'

'No. They're townies employed by the council.'

'Well, they do say that God works in mysterious ways,' Marc told him whimsically. 'And it looks as if this lady and her daughter *are* heaven-sent.'

'You bet!' Toby enthused, and when he'd gone Marc wondered if magical Mary and her daughter had husbands at home.

When he told Giselle that Frank was going ahead with the surgery, her face lit up. 'That's wonderful,' she said. 'Maybe when his groin has healed after the operation, he'll be able to wear the prosthesis again.'

The day had started well, Marc thought. There'd been the news about Frank's decison, and it was becoming clear that Giselle was beginning to feel the same sort of rapport with their patients as he did. To a lesser degree maybe, but it was there. Putting any dismal thoughts about her plans for the future to the back of his mind, he went about the day's business rejoicing.

His contentment was to be short-lived. The following day the three doctors were having a coffee at the end of morning surgery before starting the house calls when he happened to glance out of the window and saw a bright red Porsche pull onto the forecourt.

He whistled softly.There were quite a few wealthy people on his list of patients, as more and more city dwellers were moving into the countryside, but he hadn't seen this flashy number before.

Craig and Giselle, aware that something was going on outside, had crossed to his side, and as they watched the driver uncoil himself from the car, Marc saw the colour drain from Giselle's face.

'Raoul!' she gasped, and Marc thought uneasily that here might be the reason why Giselle wanted to go back to a smarter life-style. There was something about the fellow who'd just got out of the Porche that looked foreign, French possibly, and his spirits sank.

He was of medium height, had dark hair, trendily cut, and was wearing an expensive-looking suit. For a moment he stood looking around him and then began to stroll towards the door of the practice.

Giselle came to life. 'This is someone for me,' she said quickly. 'Will you excuse me for a moment?'

Marc nodded and as she hurried through Reception Craig took his spirits to an even lower level by saying, 'It figures, doesn't it, that Giselle would have a guy like that in tow?'

'No. It doesn't!' he snapped 'He could be a relation or a colleague from where she worked before.'

'Oh, yeah?' his young assistant said doubt-fully. 'Look at them!' Marc saw that the stranger had his arms around Giselle and was kissing her.

The fact that Giselle was standing stiffly in his embrace didn't register. All he could think of was that this man might be the reason why she wanted to go back to Paris.

He flinched. She was bringing him inside, for heaven's sake.

'Can I introduce a friend of mine? Raoul Antonie from Paris,' she said without meeting Marc's glance. The three men shook hands. 'I wonder if it would be possible for me to have a couple of hours away from the surgery, Marc? Raoul is driving back to London tonight and we have some catching up to do.'

He would have loved to have said no. Not because he minded her having the time off, but because he couldn't stand the thought of her being with this suave-looking character who had driven all the way from London to see her in a car that made his look as if it was ready for the scrap heap.

'Yes, of course,' he told her. 'Take the rest of the day off.'

'Thank you,' she said.

Suddenly the accent that said she was of mixed descent seemed more pronounced, and when her companion wished them a smooth *'au revoir'* it made her seem more alien than ever. Then they were gone, with the Frenchman hovering over her possessively.

The following morning Marc thought for a second time that Giselle wouldn't turn up. On the face of it she'd given him no cause to think so, yet he had a feeling of impending doom. But once again he was wrong.

She was there, already seeing her first patient when he arrived, and his heart leapt with thankfulness. At least the stranger hadn't carried her off in the night. He wondered if she was going to explain who Raoul was and why he'd turned up out of the blue. It had been clear that she hadn't been expecting him.

'Everything all right?' he asked when she

came out to put the patient's notes in the holder outside the nurses' room for treatment required.

'Yes, fine,' she said smoothly.

'Your friend get off all right?'

'Yes, thank you.'

So it was going to be like this, he thought grimly. The very private woman that he was in love with wasn't going to put him out of his misery with regard to yesterday's visitor. To someone whose life was an open book it was annoying to say the least.

But he'd reckoned without Craig. His young assistant had no qualms about asking who the caller had been, and when surgery was over he said, 'That was some trendy guy who came visiting yesterday. Do I detect a romance?'

Giselle eyed him levelly. 'That's for me to know and you to find out,' she told him. 'Raoul is someone I knew before I came here. He has a boutique in Paris and is in London on a merchandising trip.'

'And thought he would look you up while he was over here?' Marc chipped in flatly, not sure whether he should be relieved because it had been just a brief visit or should stick with his gut feeling of gloom to come.

'You have it in one,' she said coolly, determined not to let them push her into a corner.

She was still in a state of disbelief after the previous day's happenings. The thought uppermost in her mind was how she could have been attracted to the vain peacock who'd had the nerve to come strolling back into her life expecting her to be there, waiting.

'How did you find me?' she'd asked in French as she'd pointed him in the direction of Abbeyfields.

'I say your name and they say, "The doctor". Have you missed me, Giselle?'

'No. I haven't,' she'd told him decisively. 'You made your feelings clear the last time I saw you.'

'I was upset because you were leaving France and coming to this place.'

'Not as upset as I was, but one learns to adjust, Raoul. I've got friends here now who care about me, and my father is content, which means a lot.'

'But what do you find to do here?'

'Plenty. I help the village doctor to look after his patients.'

'Would that be the man who needs to see a hairstylist?'

The thought of Marc with his hair spiked up with gel was an amusing one, but she kept a straight face. 'Marc is a very busy man and hairstyling is not at the top of his list of priorities. He has a practice to run and is bringing up two children on his own.'

She didn't know why she felt compelled to defend him. Marc was quite capable of looking after himself in any situation, and she supposed she couldn't blame Raoul for classing the village as some sort of stagnant, rural backwater. It was what she'd thought herself at first.

But she was having to change her mind. It had been slowly casting its spell over her. So slowly that she hadn't been aware of it until now when she'd felt driven to defend it *and* its doctor...especially its doctor.

When she'd introduced Raoul to her father, she'd been praying her dad wouldn't refer to the younger man's 'dress shop', and he hadn't. Instead, he'd said, 'So you're the fellow who sells frocks, are you? Pleased to meet you.' She'd squirmed in silence.

Giselle had made him a meal before he'd set off back to London, and as she'd put freshly roasted ham from the butcher's, crusty new bread from the baker's and home-grown salad from James Morrison's garden centre in front of him, she hadn't been able to resist saying, 'All provided by local people. Very little of our food comes off supermarket shelves.'

When Raoul had gone, her father had said, 'So that's the boutique fellow. Will he be coming again?'

'No,' she'd told him, 'and you are an old tease with your "frocks" and "dress shops". You knew very well how to describe his business.'

'I *have* lived in Paris for a long time, you know.' He'd twinkled back at her. 'Though not in a house such as this.'

She'd smiled. 'You love this house, don't you?'

'Yes, I do. But so do you, don't you?'

'Ye-es,' she'd said slowly, 'but I still feel bad about the way I outbid Marc. I knew how badly *you* wanted it, but *he* was just as keen.'

'Well, you never know. He might live here one day when I've passed on and you've gone back to Paris,' he said. 'Or then again we might end up all living here together. You, me, Marc and the children. But that would depend on you seeing what is under your nose.' And without giving her time to reply to *that*, he'd gone to potter around in the garden.

She'd known what he'd meant, but hadn't taken him up on it. Everyone seemed determined to keep her here, except Raoul who'd thought she would be rushing back to be with him once they'd met up again.

I'm quite capable of making my own decisions, she'd thought mutinously, and when the time comes I will do just that. But deep down she'd known it would be so much easier to go back to her roots if Marc and the children hadn't been so much in her thoughts.

And now she was back at the surgery, having to deal with young Craig's curiosity and Marc's casual questioning. It had seemed like the right thing to do when she'd refused to say definitely whether she and Raoul were romantically involved. If Marc thought there was something between them, he might give up on her and then perhaps she would be able to think straight. for a change.

In the middle of the morning she saw him take a smartly dressed, sprightly looking, elderly woman into his consulting room, and when they reappeared he introduced her as 'Margaret Pollard, my mother-in-law'.

'So you're Philip Howard's daughter,' she said as keen hazel eyes looked Giselle over. 'We meet at last.'

It wasn't an unfriendly greeting, but neither was it particularly warm. There was no 'Nice to meet you' or 'I hope you are settling in all right'. Giselle had the feeling that she was being looked over and possibly found wanting.

'I've heard a lot about you from Tom and Alice, and Marc has mentioned you,' she said. 'Those two children *do* need a younger woman in their lives but, please, don't raise their hopes if you aren't going to be around long.'

Marc had been called to one side by the practice manager and didn't hear that. Giselle wished he had. It seemed that she was mistaken in thinking he hadn't discussed her with his mother-in-law and annoyance was warming her blood.

What was wrong with everyone that they were so interested in her comings and goings? she thought angrily. It wouldn't be so bad if she'd given them any cause to think she was anxious to take the place of Marc's dead wife. She hadn't. Yet she was still being seen as an opportunist, and who more than anyone was going to have something to say about it than Amanda's mother?

'I think your grandchildren are adorable,

Mrs Pollard. I would never do anything to upset them,' she said stiffly. 'If you want me to keep away from them, I will. Just as long as you are prepared to tell them why.

'I thought that I was settling down in this place, getting used to the closeness of your community, but instead of that I'm beginning to feel claustrophobic because of the way my affairs are of such interest to everyone. Marc and I have already discussed my presence in his children's lives and I thought we understood each other, but it would seem that I was wrong.'

'I was merely passing on a word of warning,' Margaret said, and with a wave to the receptionists she went.

When Marc turned back to where they'd been standing and saw that she'd gone, he said, 'That was quick. Margaret has been saying she wanted to meet you and as she had to pop in for a prescription for Stanley. I thought it was as good an opportunity as any. However, she must have been in a rush.'

'It was more a case of having said her piece,

there was nothing left to stay for,' Giselle told him stonily.

'And what is that supposed to mean?' he asked, as the chill in her voice registered.

'I've just been told to keep away from Tom and Alice as if I have hidden motives. Why everyone here is so interested in *my* boring life, I really don't know, but it is obvious that you've been discussing me with her.'

'You're wrong,' he said with ominous calm. 'I haven't discussed you with anyone. I know how prickly you are about that kind of thing.'

'Prickly! That's the first time I've heard wanting some privacy described in that way. And if *you* haven't been talking about me to your mother-in-law, who has? I was beginning to get a feeling of belonging here, but now I find that I'm being looked at with distrust.'

She watched his jawline tighten.

'Not by me, you aren't,' he said levelly. 'You're the best thing that has happened to the practice in a long time.'

She was the best thing that had happened to

him, too, but it was not the moment to tell her *that*, he thought wryly as he went on to say, 'It is unforgivable if you're being made to feel the way you describe, and I can only apologise on everyone's behalf.

'Margaret is a very forthright person. She would be protecting her chicks and I have no quarrel with that, but I won't allow her to do it at your expense. I shall have words with her when I see her this evening.'

He was treading carefully. It would be so easy to tell Giselle that he was in love with her. That if she ever felt the same he would be in heaven on earth. That he and his children would welcome her into their lives with open arms. But the chances of that were becoming more remote by the minute.

For one thing there was glamour boy in the background. She hadn't come up with a straight answer when Craig had asked if they were involved in a relationship. Though if they were, she hadn't exactly been starry-eyed when he'd turned up. But he'd already discovered that Giselle didn't display her feelings for all to see, except when she was angry, like now.

If she hadn't had this fixation about everyone interfering in her life, he would have had a word with her father. He liked Philip Howard and might have found out from him if she *was* involved with the Frenchman. His appearance the previous day had shown that her ties with the life she had left behind were not completely broken. But after his mother-in-law's intervention there was no way he could ask Giselle's father about her private life.

'Has it occurred to you that Margaret must chat to your father when she drops Tom and Alice off each day? They know each other from way back, don't they?' he pointed out. "He might have mentioned how you are fond of the children and set her off on the warpath.'

Giselle had listened to him without interruption. But now, with her colour rising, she said, 'I'm sorry for flying off at you like I did, Marc. Maybe you're right. My father is someone else who wants me to stay here, but if it was he who told your mother-in-law how well I get on with the children, I can understand her feelings. I've told you what my plans are and nothing has changed.'

A discreet cough from the doorway behind them indicated that if they weren't ready to start the house visits, Craig was, and within minutes the three doctors were going out to their cars.

Giselle wasn't doing the rounds with Marc now that she knew the area and was more familiar with the patients, but each day he wished that she was. Today in particular so that they could have carried on the conversation that Craig had brought to an end.

Yet what was there left to say? She had been adamant that nothing had changed regarding her plans, and unless a miracle happened he was going to lose the love of his life.

If he was on his own, without children, he would act differently. Pursue her, woo her, make her see what a good life they could have together. But the scales weren't evenly balanced. If Giselle ever did return his feelings, it would have to be because she wanted him as much as he wanted her. Not because of his selfish motives.

Travelling in the opposite direction, Giselle was experiencing relief rather than frustration. She felt that she'd just made a fool of herself twice over. Firstly, she'd accused Marc of somethng he hadn't done. She had only known him for a short time, but had already got the measure of the man, and knew instinctively that he wouldn't lie.

Her second act of foolishness had been to once again reaffirm that she did not intend to stay in England. It might be the place of her birth, but it was not where she'd lived all her life. Why did she have to keep harping on about it? If ever she changed her mind, she would look like a fool after all her protestations.

Marc must be tired of her playing the same old tune from the same old record. He wasn't to know that she'd been on the point of faltering in her determination, and he was the reason. But that had been before she'd met the redoubtable Margaret and had been warned off.

Yet upset as she was, she understood. The woman cared devotedly for Tom and Alice while their father was running the practice. If she was fiercely protective of them, who could blame her? She hoped that Marc wouldn't take Margaret to task on *her* account.

Her first call of the day was to Irene's house and Giselle thought that her chat didn't seem to have done the trick as she'd demanded a visit as soon as possible.

It seemed to be taking her a long time to answer the door and when at last it swung open, Irene was framed there on hands and knees, looking absolutely dreadful, and Giselle knew that at last the woman had her wish. She was ill.

'What's wrong?' she asked, helping her distressed patient slowly to her feet.

'I don't know,' Irene groaned. 'It struck me

in the middle of the night when I was going to the bathroom. I couldn't walk and I've been on my hands and knees ever since. I live on my own. There's nobody to look after me. I need to go to hospital.'

'Not until I've examined you,' Giselle told her. 'Have you been having trouble getting out of bed in the mornings?'

'Yes. It's been really difficult.'

'I thought so. I'm going to do what is called an ESR blood test. It will show if you have any inflammation. I shall take it back to the surgery as soon as I've done it, so that it will get to the lab today.'

'So what's wrong with me?' Irene asked, as the old fascination began to come back now that she was receiving attention.

'It could be polymyalgia rheumatica,' Giselle informed her. 'Inflammation of the muscles. It is an illness that surfaces in women over fifty and is supposed to be rare, but I've seen it a few times. At its onset it is very painful, but once the patient is put on steroids, it improves rapidly.

'There won't be any need for you to be hospitalised if it is what I think. But the steroids will have to be monitored very carefully, which means I will have to see you frequently.'

Irene was cheering up by the minute. 'I've always wanted to be on steroids,' she said.

Would she be as happy about the weight gain, moon face and unwanted hair that the magical treatment could cause? Giselle wondered. But a diagnosis had yet to be made and once she'd taken the blood she went back to the surgery to arrange for it to be sent off to be tested with all speed.

As she was about to get into her car for a second time to continue her rounds, the sound of children's voices attracted her attention, and when she looked up a long line of pupils from the village school were passing on their way to some outdoor pursuit.

They looked about the right age for Alice's class and as she scanned their faces, sure enough, she was there, waving and smiling, pointing proudly to a gap in her teeth that hadn't been there the previous day when the children had come to play.

Tenderness washed over her. Alice was a sweet, uncomplicated child. It was taking her all her time not to rush across and give her a hug, but apart from the fact that it wouldn't go down too well with her teacher, Giselle hadn't forgotten her grandmother's comments of the day before and when her day at the surgery had been over she'd purposely hung back so that Marc and herself had arrived at Abbeyfields together, leaving no time for her to be with the children.

He hadn't missed the ploy and had said brusquely, 'There is no need for you to start avoiding Alice and Tom. It will upset them more than anything if you suddenly drop out of their lives while you're still around.'

She'd sighed. 'I can't do right for doing wrong, can I? I love being with them, but I have to respect what their grandma said. I can see her point of view. I can see everyone's points of view, hers, yours, my father's, but no one seems to be able to see mine.'

'I do,' he'd said in the same abrupt tone. 'If I didn't, you would be seeing a lot more of me.'

'What? More than I do already?' she'd mocked.

'Yes. A lot more.' And on that note he'd collected the children and gone.

Giselle was on a house call to a cottage halfway up a hillside. A young couple had bought it recently and had immediately registered with the practice. The young woman was now pregnant.

Today there'd been a phone call, asking for a visit, as she was experiencing stomach pains, and that was where Giselle was heading. Until she saw a still figure lying beneath a steep drop from one of the overhanging peaks.

Pulling to the side of the dirt track that she'd just turned onto, she was out of the car in a flash and bending over a middle-aged man in walking clothes. He was alive, conscious, and his face was as green as the grass that he lay on. When she bent over him he groaned, 'My legs! I think they're broken.'

'Hold on there,' she said, and ran back to the car for her case and her phone. 'What happened?' she asked, crouching beside him again.

'I was walking along the tops, enjoying the scenery and the fresh air, when I heard the sound of hoofs behind me and saw a herd of wild deer heading straight towards me. I stepped sideways in a panic, forgetting how near the edge I was, and as they veered away I went over.'

She nodded. 'All right. I'm a doctor. Don't move.'

'I couldn't if I wanted to,' he told her weakly. 'And thank goodness for that.'

'What?'

'That you're a doctor.'

'I'm going to ring for an ambulance first and then I'll see just how badly hurt you are. Any pain in the back?'

'Yes, plenty. I wouldn't be surprised if I'd broken it.'

With an ambulance on its way, Giselle began to assess how badly hurt the man was.

'I'm going to give you an injection to relieve the pain,' she told him gently, 'and then I'm going to cut away your trousers to examine your legs.'

Both knees were shattered so it would appear that as he'd crumpled in landing they'd gone beneath him and taken the full weight of the fall. But she thought sombrely it could have been even worse if he hadn't fallen onto the grass verge beside the rough track.

The injured man was lapsing in and out of consciousness now and she checked her watch anxiously. It had only been ten minutes since she'd called the ambulance service. They wouldn't be here yet, though she could hear the sound of a car engine. When she looked up, Giselle's eyes widened. It was Marc's car that was coming towards her.

'What's happened?' he asked as he flung

himself out of the driver's seat. 'I saw your car as I was driving past the end of the lane.'

'The man was walking on the tops and was startled by a herd of deer racing along behind him. He sidestepped and fell over the edge.'

'He should have known that they're shy creatures and would be more scared of him than he was of them.'

'Maybe he isn't a regular country dweller, *like myself*,' she said as Marc dropped to his knees and felt the man's pulse.

'His heartbeat seems regular enough,' she told him, 'but with these sorts of injuries there is no telling for how long.'

At that moment the injured walker opened his eyes and mumbled, 'The ramblers…they'll be wondering where I've got to.'

'So you weren't alone?' Giselle asked.

'No. I'd wandered off from the group. They don't move fast enough for me.'

'What do we do about that?' she asked Marc.

'Nothing,' he said calmly. 'They'll go back to base most likely, thinking that he's still ahead of them. Soon enough for them to find out that he isn't then. By which time he will be in A and E. They'll be informed of that when they ring the police. *Our* main concern is to get this poor fellow seen to.' They heard a siren in the distance. 'Maybe this is the ambulance now.'

It was, and once the patient's legs had been strapped together to prevent movement and he'd been lifted onto a spinal board, the ambulance was off, speeding along to where the resources of the hospital were waiting.

'How was it that you came across him?' Marc asked when they'd gone.

'I was on my way to the cottage at the end of this lane,' she told him. 'A woman four months pregnant with stomach pains. I hope that she'll forgive the delay.'

'Right. I'll be off, then,' he said. 'But before I go, I wondered if you would like to come round for Sunday lunch.'

Giselle could feel her jaw dropping. What was he thinking of?

'Thank you for the invitation but no,' she said. 'I would have expected that to be the last thing you would be suggesting after what your mother-in-law said yesterday.'

'That is the reason why I'm asking,' he told her with a wry smile. 'I know that Margaret upset you and I want to make amends.'

'And you think that's the way?' she exclaimed. 'It will make matters worse, not better.'

'It will show Margaret and everyone else who might be interested that *I* decide what I do with my life. Just as you are so determined to do what you want with yours. And in any case, one Sunday lunch isn't going to make the children pine for you any more when you leave. So what do you say?'

The memory of Alice waving to her and smiling her gappy smile came back and Giselle couldn't resist the opportunity to be with her and Tom in *their* family setting for a change.

'All right, then,' she agreed. 'You've talked me into it.'

There was nothing wry about his smile now.

It was a delighted beam. 'Great!' he said, adding with a twinkle in his eye, 'Are you any good with a tin opener?'

The young woman who'd asked for the visit flashed Giselle an apologetic smile when she opened the door to her. 'I think it was just a gastric upset,' she said. 'The pain has gone, Doctor. I've been on and off the toilet for the last hour and it's gone.'

'That's good, Sarah,' Giselle told her, 'but I think I'd better examine you to be on the safe side. Has there been any bleeding?'

'No.'

'None at all?'

'No. None.'

'All right, that sounds reassuring, but I want to make sure that your uterus and cervix are how they should be at this stage in your pregnancy so if you would like to take off your panties and tights, I'll examine you.'

When she'd finished Giselle told the young mother-to-be, 'Everything seems fine. I think you are right about the gastric upset, but don't be lulled into a feeling of false confidence. Any spotting or stomach cramps, send for me immediately.'

'I will,' Sarah said fervently. 'It's my first baby and I don't want to lose it. I'm so glad to find a woman doctor at the practice. I don't remember you being mentioned when we joined.'

'How long ago was it?' Giselle asked.

'Six months.'

'I wasn't there then. I've only been in this country for a short time.'

'Where did you live before?'

'Paris.'

'Ooh! Lucky you!' the girl exclaimed.

When the door closed behind her Giselle stood without moving for a moment.

Yes. She was lucky to have lived in Paris, she thought. But would she feel as lucky if she went back there and left behind a certain doctor and his children *and* turned her back on the engrossing, never-the-same-for-two-moments-together life of a country GP?

CHAPTER SEVEN

THE good news on Frank Fairbank's operation was that the cancer hadn't spread. The bad news was that he was to be given radio-therapy to prevent it from returning and was going to have to use crutches until the skin had healed from both the operation and the treatment.

When Toby phoned the surgery to say that his father was home, Marc went to see him and was admitted to the farmhouse by a pleasant elderly woman who introduced herself as Mary, the home help.

As he looked around him he was reminded of what Toby had said regarding this woman's influence in the all-male household. It was indeed a transformation she had brought about, and at what better time than when Frank was likely to be at his lowest?

'Frank is in the sitting room,' she told him. 'I've just made some tea. Would you like a cup, Doctor?'

"I'd love one,' he told her, with the memory of Toby saying what a joy it would be to find a clean cup. From the looks of this woman, there would be an abundance of clean everything, he thought, and that, if nothing else, should make Frank feel better.

His patient was seated by the window, doing a crossword, when Marc went in, and his smile *was* that of a happier man as he said, 'Morning, Dr Bannerman.'

'So how are you, Frank?' Marc asked.

'I'm sore from the radiotherapy,' the farmer replied, 'and until it has healed I won't be able to wear my leg.' He pointed to the prosthesis, lying on the chest of drawers beside him with a big satin bow tied around it, and laughed. 'That's a bit of Mary. She keeps me cheerful.'

'I can see that,' Marc told him. 'And what

about her daughter? Is she still coming to help keep the place tidy?'

'Yes. *She* keeps that lad of mine cheerful, too.'

'It sounds as if you've found yourselves two treasures,' Marc said lightly. 'But don't they have families of their own to look after?'

'Naw. Mary is a widow and Denise isn't married. She lives with her mother.'

'I see,' Marc said slowly.

'Naw, you don't,' Frank told him dryly. 'Them two women wouldn't look at us. Me with only one leg, an' Toby always up to his ears in pig swill.'

'Not all the time, surely,' Marc teased. 'And if you should be short of a best man, I'll be only too willing to oblige.'

'Get away with you!' Frank replied, and then lapsed into silence as Mary came in with the tea.

When they'd drunk the steaming brew Marc said, 'And now, Frank, I'd like to see what they've done at your groin.'

'That's neat,' he said, when he'd examined

where the surgery had taken place. 'It looks just the same as it did before, except for a small scar and the soreness from the radiotherapy. That will disappear eventually and then it will be time to undo the satin bow and get mobile again.'

"I hope so.' Frank said. 'I really do hope so!'

When Giselle arrived at Marc's house for Sunday lunch, Alice, pink-cheeked with excitement, took her hand and pulled her inside, telling her breathlessly, '*I've* set the table, Giselle.' She pointed to her brother hovering in the kitchen doorway. 'And Tom has shelled the peas and chopped up the carrots.'

'My goodness!' Giselle exclaimed laughingly. 'I *am* honoured.'

'You should be,' Marc said, appearing behind his son. 'You're our first guest since the children lost their mother.'

'Am I really?' she said gravely, determined not to read too much into *that*. 'Then I am indeed honoured.'

He was smiling, but she knew there'd been a message for her in what he'd said, which made his comment when he'd asked her to come to lunch seem rather understated.

'One Sunday lunch won't make any difference,' he'd said when she'd reminded him of his mother-in-law's remarks. But he hadn't told her that she would be their first visitor since they'd lost Amanda, which put a different slant on the occasion.

But she was there now and was deciding that nothing was going to spoil it for the children. They were obviously pleased to see her and excited to be entertaining a visitor. She wasn't going to put a foot wrong.

Marc's voice interrupted her thoughts.

'Are you any good at making gravy?' he was asking. 'I know the rudiments of it, but it usually turns out lumpy, and the French are supposed to be such good cooks.'

There was laughter in his voice and when she followed him into the kitchen she saw that a succulent joint of beef had been cooked to perfection and she could see Yorkshire puddings through the glass door of the oven.

'If you can make Yorkshire puddings, you should be able to make gravy,' she said, acutely conscious of his nearness as he stood beside her, wearing a big plastic apron.

'They're bought, I'm afraid,' he confessed. 'As are the trifles and profiteroles that we're having for dessert, but everything else is home-cooked.'

'It all looks delicious,' she said, smiling up at him.

He didn't return her smile. There was a look in his eyes that made her feel as if an unseen force had taken hold of them and was welding them together. She'd only seen it once before, but wasn't ever going to forget it. It had been in this house that he'd kissed her and during those moments in his arms everything else in her life had receded.

'So shall we make the gravy?' she croaked.

As if Marc had been somewhere far away, he said absently, 'Er...yes.'

The children kept the conversation going during the meal and Giselle was glad of it. It registered vaguely that the food was very good, that Tom and Alice were lively but well behaved *and* that Marc was still sending out the message that she'd picked up on in the kitchen.

It was unfair of him to do this to her, she thought. It was supposed to be family lunch. What had got into him?

'Stop it!' she told him when the children had gone into the garden to play and he and she were clearing away after the meal.

'Stop what?'

'Don't pretend you don't know what I mean, Marc, ' she snapped. 'You've got me here under false pretences.'

'Have I laid a finger on you? No. So what do you mean, Giselle?'

'I mean that you don't have to touch me with your hands. Your eyes are doing it for you. Every time I looked at you during the meal it felt as if you were caressing me.'

'And you don't want that?'

'No! Yes! I don't know whether I do or I don't. You are deliberately confusing me and it isn't fair. You led me to believe it was going to be an innocent family lunch.'

He sighed.

'Yes, I know, and I'm sorry. I wasn't prepared for the effect you had on me the moment I saw you.'

'You've seen me often enough before.'

'Not here, I haven't. You've been here just once and it was the memory of that other time that came back so vividly when you were standing close to me in the kitchen. 'I want to make love to you, Giselle, so much that I can't think straight. I've never felt this way about any other woman in the whole of my life.'

'What about your wife? Didn't you feel like that about *her*?'

'No. I'll tell you about Amanda some time.'

Her heart was thudding in her breast. 'And if I say yes, where do we go from there? You know I'm not intending on staying in the village. What do you have in mind? An affair?

Are you suggesting that we pop upstairs and hope the children don't disturb us?'

She couldn't believe she was discussing this overwhelming attraction between them so coldly. But she knew that if Marc so much as touched her at this moment she would stop fighting it and give in.

His expression was indicating that she'd gone too far.

'No, I do not want an affair,' he said tightly, as the heat drained from him. 'I would want a much bigger commitment from you than that, and if you think that I would risk my children walking in on us, you don't know me very well.

'For goodness' sake, go back to where you came from, Giselle. I'm weary of hearing you tell me that you're not staying. And if the big attraction over there is that…that gigolo who came to see you the other day, the best of luck!'

'You…are…insulting,' she said in slow anger. 'I'm going!'

'After you've said goodbye to the children, I hope.'

'Of course. How could you think otherwise?'

'Just checking, that's all.'

Engrossed in their play, Tom and Alice didn't pick up any bad vibes from her departure and waved her off serenely. As for their father, he had nothing further to say. He watched her depart with the tight expression still there and then went back inside to ponder about what had happened.

There was no way that Giselle wanted to go home and face her father's questions as to why she was back so soon. She needed to be where she could sort out the chaos of her thoughts, and where better than up on the moors in the space and silence. Space and silence! Not so long ago she would have run a mile from such timeless rural splendour.

Marc had given her her marching orders, she thought furiously as she drove up the road that led to the tops. How dared he? All right, maybe she had said she wasn't intending to stay once too often, but who was he to tell her when to go and when to stay?

She wasn't in a position to go anywhere yet. Her father was happy to be back in Abbeyfields and amongst his old haunts, but she wanted to see him looking more robust before she made any moves of her own.

They'd both gone countless nights without sleep during the last months of her mother's illness and Celeste's last request to her daughter had been that she take care of her father.

The clear country air and quieter surroundings were already working to good effect. Philip didn't look as pale and skeletal as when he'd first come back, but Giselle wanted to go with an easy mind when she went, and after today she wasn't all that sure that she still wanted to go.

Easy mind! she thought. What was an easy mind? She'd met a man in the same profession as herself, which automatically would have created a degree of rapport between them, but she knew deep down that if Marc had been the butcher, the baker or even the candlestick maker, she would have been attracted to him.

But he was happy *here*. He was content to spend his days in the place he loved best, and she couldn't blame him for that. He had two young children to consider, who were happy and well adjusted in spite of losing their mother, and credit for some of that was due to the woman who had said her piece the other day at the practice.

And now he'd just told her baldly to go back to where she'd come from if she was so keen to return there. Yet in contradiction to that he was making it harder with each passing day for her to fight the attraction between them.

She'd been so aware of him back there in his house, so aroused by the messages he'd been giving out, that nothing else had seemed to matter, except that she wanted him as much as he wanted her

When she pulled in beside a steep drop, with only a stray sheep for company, Giselle rested her head on the steering-wheel and wept. If only *maman* was here to open her heart to, she thought wretchedly. Yet she knew that if her mother had still been alive, there would have been no problem. Her father would have been happy to stay in France and *she* wouldn't be out here in the wilds, trying to sort out her life.

How long she'd been there, she didn't know. As a September sun began to sink below the horizon someone tapped on the car window, and when she looked up Giselle saw the weather-beaten face of an elderly farmer peering at her through the glass.

'Are you all right, miss?' he asked when she wound down the window.

'Er…yes…I'm fine,' she told him unconvincingly.

His glance was on the steep drop beside the car and she realised that he was thinking that she might be suicidal. 'Only you was here when I passed a while back,' he said.

'I'm fine,' she repeated. 'I just needed some time to myself.'

He nodded. 'Aye, I can understand that. You young 'uns never let up, do you?' He was peering closer. 'Wait a minute, though! Aren't you the new doctor from the surgery down there?'

'Yes.'

'Then I take back what I've just said. If there's one lot of people who can be excused for being busy, it's you lot. Dr Bannerman in particular. Us folks in these parts are lucky to have somebody as on the ball as he is, sorting out our aches and pains.'

Giselle sighed. She'd come up here to get away from Marc, but it was not to be. Even up here on this deserted moorland road she'd met someone who wanted to talk about him.

'However, I'd better get on,' he said to her relief, 'It was just that I drove past earlier, and when I saw that you were still here I thought I'd better stop and see if you were all right.'

It was here again, she thought. The caring community that she'd so reluctantly become a part of. This man might live on the far fringes of the village but he was still one of them.

He'd let the desire to make love supersede that of making the gravy, Marc thought with bleak humour when she'd gone. Everything had been fine until Giselle had come to stand beside him in the kitchen, and then it had been there again, the ache inside him, the longing to hold her close in passion and tenderness. But instead of keeping his feelings in check, he'd let them take over and then, when she hadn't been ready to fall panting into his arms, he had told her to go back to where she'd come from.

As the children played happily in the garden, he wandered restlessly from room to room. He'd never looked at another woman since losing Amanda, had never been even remotely attracted to one, until Giselle had appeared on the scene, and now all the joyous wonder of falling deeply in love was taking him nowhere. Why couldn't he have been attracted to some uncomplicated local woman who was less reserved than Giselle and with no longing to be somewhere else?

He'd given the children their tea and, still furious with himself for spoiling Sunday lunch with Giselle, had just decided that he had to see her again before the day was out when the phone rang.

'Philip Howard here, Marc,' the voice said apologetically. 'Call me an old fusspot, but is Giselle still with you? She said she would be back by late afternoon and I've been thinking that either she's enjoying herself so much with you and the children that she has lost track of time or that she's gone somewhere else without letting me know, which isn't like her.'

'Giselle isn't here, Philip,' Marc said slowly. 'She left hours ago and I assumed that she was returning to Abbeyfields.'

'Then I wonder where she can be,' Philip fretted as Marc had a vision of a flight to Paris taking off with Giselle on board. Yet he knew she wouldn't do that. She took her responsibilities too seriously to leave her father without a word. Unless he, like the tactless fool that he was, had driven her to do something completely out of character.

'Her mobile appears to be switched off, so I'm not going to be able to contact her that way,' Philip was saying.

'I'll come over,' Marc told him, uneasy now. 'I'll have to bring the children with me, and will be with you shortly.'

It was dark now, and as he bundled Alice and Tom into the car his feelings of guilt were weighing him down. Yet why should he think that Giselle's disappearance had anything to do with him? he thought uncomfortably. Wasn't he overestimating his importance in her life?

Philip was waiting for them on the porch and his first words were, 'Still no sign of Giselle, Marc.'

He didn't need to be told that, Marc thought. Her father's expression and the fact that Giselle's car was nowhere to be seen were proof enough.

Alice was tugging at his sleeve as they went

inside and asked, 'Why have we come to Giselle's house instead of going to bed?'

'I'll explain later, Alice,' he told her. 'Why don't you both go to watch TV for a while, if Mr Howard doesn't mind?'

'I don't mind at all,' Giselle's father told them. 'There are some biscuits in a tin in the kitchen if you're hungry.'

At that moment the phone rang, and when he picked it up his face went slack with relief.

'It's her,' he said. 'Giselle has been for a drive and is on her way back. She'll be home in a few minutes.' And then, as if he'd been asked a question, he said into the phone, 'I'm talking to Marc, my dear. He came round when he realised that you hadn't come home.' There was a pause and then he said, 'Maybe it *wasn't* necessary, but that was what he preferred to do. Yes, all right. I'll tell him.'

'She says there's no need to wait,' he explained when he'd replaced the receiver. 'She's fine and doesn't want to trouble you further.'

Marc nodded. He was getting the message

loud and clear. Wherever it was that she'd been, Giselle didn't want *him* on the scene when she got back.

'We'll be off, then,' he told her father. 'Giselle will probably have a good explanation for being absent when she gets in. The main thing is that now your mind is at rest.'

On that note he collected the children from in front of the television, tucked them into the car once more and drove back home, with no delusions regarding Giselle's feelings towards him.

'I'm so sorry I didn't phone earlier to let you know where I was,' Giselle told her father contritely when she arrived home.

He smiled. 'I'll let you off this once, but where were you? I rang Marc to ask if you were still there and he said you'd left hours ago, so I became concerned.'

Giselle sighed. 'We'd had a disagreement. I drove up to the moors to cool off and didn't realise what time it was until the sun began to go down.'

Her father was frowning. 'I thought you got on well with Marc.'

'I do… I did… It is just that Marc wants me to stay here permanently.'

'And why would that be? Because he's attracted to you?'

'Something like that.'

'And you don't feel the same way?'

'I don't know what I feel.'

'If you want him enough you'll stay, Giselle. It is as simple as that. But only you can decide. I wouldn't try to influence you either way. You do know that, don't you?'

She gave him a quick squeeze. 'Yes. I do. At least I know where I stand with you.'

'That's because I'm your father.' He smiled at his daughter. 'Marc's a fine man, you know. They don't come any finer, but I've just said that I won't influence you, haven't I?'

Giselle laughed. 'So speaks another member of the Marc Bannerman appreciation society. Even an old farmer I met up on the moors was part of his fan club. I can't help feeling there's a conspiracy afoot to keep me here.'

'No way,' her father protested. 'You have a mind of your own and will make your own decision when the time comes. Don't hang on here because of me, Giselle. I'm fine now that I've settled in. All I want is for you to be happy and I feel I should have given *that* more consideration when I sent you over here to bid for Abbeyfields.'

"I wouldn't have wanted it to be any different,' she told him gently, 'and I'm not going anywhere yet. It is just that I wasn't expecting to meet someone like Marc when I came here.'

'So are you going to stay on at the surgery if there is friction between you?' her father asked.

'Yes, if he wants me to after yesterday's exchange of words. What would I find to do otherwise? And I enjoy being a country GP.'

'Is Giselle angry with us?' Alice asked when they arrived back home. 'She didn't want to see us, did she?'

'Not with you and Tom, she isn't. Giselle would never be angry with you guys,' he told her gently, 'but I'm afraid that she isn't too pleased with me.'

'Why?' Alice wanted to know.

'Because I want her to stay here in the village with us.'

Alice's face crumpled. 'Nobody told *us* that she was going away.'

'It won't be happening for a while. Not until she thinks that Mr Howard is well enough to be left on his own,' he told her consolingly, thinking that he hadn't been wrong in expecting his children to be just as miserable as he would be to see her go. But at least they were getting a gentle warning, which would prepare them for when the time came.

'She could be our mum if she stayed,' Tom said, as his contribution to the discussion.

'We could ask her,' Alice said, brightening at the thought. 'We could tell Giselle that we would always be good and wouldn't cause any trouble.'

If Marc had been miserable before, this conversation with his two precious children was taking his gloom into new depths. That they should be prepared to make such promises to keep Giselle in their lives was heartbreaking. The three of them had been content before she'd appeared, jogging along as best they could but now everything had changed.

Panic was setting in as he thought that the worst possible thing that could happen would be for Tom and Alice to say their piece to her. The idea that Giselle might think he was using his children to plead his case was making him break out in a sweat.

He put his arms around them both, held them close and told them, 'I know that we want to be happy and would love it if Giselle stayed here. But we would want her to be happy, too, wouldn't we?' They both nodded solemnly and he went on, 'And that might mean her going back to where she came from. So I don't want either of you to say anything to her. She has to make up her own mind.'

He wasn't to know that her father was saying

that very same thing to Giselle in the house that he had once hoped would be his. Neither did he know that *he* had been the main topic of their conversation since she'd returned after all those hours up on the moors, and that the vision of a small, smart apartment in Paris that she'd been holding on to ever since leaving France was being blotted out by his face, his voice, his charisma, everything that was Marc Bannerman.

'Now, do you hear me, children?' he said firmly. 'Not a word to Giselle…please. And as it is school tomorrow and Monday mornings are the most hectic of the week, I think that it's time you were both tucked up in bed. And don't forget what I said, not a word to Giselle.'

'We promise,' they chorused in subdued small voices and Marc thought miserably that he should never have allowed Tom and Alice to be affected by his crazy passion for Giselle. It had to stop, and he vowed that from now on *he* would keep *her* at arm's length. He would do it, even if it tore him apart.

* * *

Marc had already thought twice before that Giselle wouldn't turn up for surgery the day after they'd had some sort of confrontation, and had the same feeling this time. But Giselle was there on Monday morning, before him as usual, looking pale and heavy-eyed.

Under normal circumstances Marc would have asked if she was all right, but not today. He was pretty sure why she looked as she did and knew that he was to blame.

As the day progressed he was also aware that she was avoiding him. Sticking to his resolve of the night before, he did the same with her and spoke to her only if he had to.

'Do I detect an atmosphere?' Craig asked when Giselle took her coffee into her room instead of joining them as she usually did before they set off on their home visits.

Marc didn't answer. He swallowed his own drink down quickly and within seconds was pointing his car towards his first call of the day.

* * *

As September crept slowly by with its mellow days and chillier nights, the stand-off between the two doctors continued. The children still came round to play in the fields after school. Their father still came to pick them up, but didn't linger. Tom and Alice played happily enough but Giselle was aware of a feeling of withdrawal, as if the rapport she'd had with them had gone. They didn't have much to say and when they had it was said with a sort of uncomfortable politeness, which made her think that Marc had warned them that she was just someone passing through their lives.

If he had, she couldn't blame him. If she had been in his place she would have done the same, but it didn't stop her from being hurt by their restraint. They'd been so natural and friendly towards her, and the fact that they had no mother had made her feel tender and protective towards them.

As their grandmother had said that day when she'd called in at the surgery, they needed a younger woman in their lives, but not one whose hopes and plans were centred around a place far away.

Giselle kept telling herself that if she were to admit that she was in love with Marc, there would be no chance of history repeating itself. Her father had gone to live in France to please her mother, and workwise it hadn't been too difficult. He'd transferred to his firm's French office and been happy enough. Yet it hadn't stopped him from wanting to come back home once her mother had died.

But for Marc it would be very different. He wouldn't want to uproot his children from the life that they knew, where they were happy and secure. And he was a doctor in a country practice that was very dear to his heart.

There was another solution, of course. A simple one that she kept shelving. She hoped it wasn't connected with selfishness. That her reluctance to accept it was because right from the start she'd been loth to leave Paris, and for anyone other than her father would have refused to do so.

After losing her mother, she'd needed familiar surroundings to help cushion her grief and had been dismayed to discover that their loss was affecting him in the opposite way. He'd wanted to come back home, and how could she have refused him that after all that he'd gone through?

In the middle of the gloom came a ray of light. Not in *their* lives but in the lives of others who'd had their share of trouble. It was all round the village. There was going to be a double wedding. Father and son were to marry mother and daughter, and everyone was agog at the news.

'It was love at first sight,' Frank told Marc when he called to see how he was progressing. 'Neither of us, Toby nor me, had ever thought any women would fancy us. Me because I've only got one leg and am past my sell-by date, and that lad of mine has always been so bogged down with this place he's never had the chance to meet any. But Mary and Denise must have seen us in a different light,' he said, his cheeks reddening. 'We're going to divide this place in two, but we're not delaying the wedding for that. I told Mary that once I'd managed to get this leg of mine back where it belonged, I'd be ready to walk down the aisle. And see.' He held his leg and patted it lovingly. 'There it is!'

As Marc was on the point of leaving Frank had said, 'Would you fancy doing us a favour?'

Marc smiled, delighted that for once things were going right for this tough old man and his son.

'Yes, if I can.'

'Do you remember what you once said about if we needed a best man? Well, how about it? Will you be best man...for both of us?'

'I can't think of anything I would enjoy more,' Marc told him.

CHAPTER EIGHT

MARC'S step was light when he arrived back at the surgery. There was going to be a village wedding and he and the children were to be part of it. He was ready for something to break the monotony of life without Giselle.

'Bring those children of yours,' Frank had said, 'and a partner for yourself.'

He'd asked if Marc thought his father-in-law would be well enough to attend and he'd replied, 'Possibly, but Stanley's not the man he was. He has decided to retire and, as you know, I have a temporary doctor working with me at the moment.'

How temporary he wasn't sure as communication between Giselle and himself was still limited since he'd told her to go back to Paris.

Thankfully she hadn't yet taken him up on it, but there was always the dread in him that she would suddenly confront him and announce her departure.

But today he was on a high and Mollie said, 'You look on top of the world, Dr Bannerman.'

He smiled. 'I am, Mollie. Frank and Toby Fairbank have asked me to be best man at their weddings.'

'Now, that *is* nice,' she said, and it was. Just as long as he didn't keep reminding himself that in the present climate it was the nearest he was ever going to get to the altar of the old village church that dated back to Norman times.

'What about the leg? Frank's leg?' Giselle asked. She'd come in from behind him and when he swivelled round she was standing in the doorway of her consulting room.

'He was wearing it when I called,' he told her, taking in the vision that never failed to make his blood warm. 'Frank had decided that he wasn't getting married until he could walk down the aisle, and hopefully that's what he'll be doing.'

'The children are invited to the wedding and I've been told to bring a partner.' On the spur of the moment, he said casually, 'Would you feel like doing the honours?'

He'd deliberately asked her in front of Mollie. That way they wouldn't start getting into personalities, just as long as Giselle was prepared to give him a straight answer.

Marc held his breath. He'd asked her on impulse and was expecting a refusal, but she was smiling.

'Yes,' she said. 'I haven't been to a wedding in ages. From what I've been told, those two men haven't had much happiness in recent years, so it will be a pleasure to see their lives take on new meaning.'

She didn't meet his glance and Marc wondered if she was aware how much 'new meaning' she could bring to his life if she would only change her mind.

He wasn't to know that Giselle had endured enough of the cold silences and infrequent conversations. She was desperate for an opening that would bring them back into each other's lives, and he'd just given her one.

The sparkle had come back into the beautiful violet eyes that had been the first thing he had noticed about her. Her body was more relaxed than it had been in weeks. But he told himself that every woman liked a wedding, and as if to confirm the thought she said, 'Would you like me to take Alice to buy a new dress when I go for an outfit for myself? Or would you prefer that her grandma took her?'

'I'm sure that Margaret wouldn't mind, and I certainly wouldn't,' he said immediately. 'My mother-in-law's tastes are somewhat staid, and even at *her* tender age Alice knows what's in fashion for six-year-olds.'

He couldn't believe it, he was thinking crazily. They were almost back on track. Risking a rebuff, he suggested, 'Why don't we all go together so that Tom and I can get fixed up at the same time? He won't be terribly excited about having to be dressed up on the day, but he'll enjoy the outing if we all go together.'

As he waited for her reply he was thinking that what he'd just said had overtones of pleading, and that was the last thing he'd intended. If ever Giselle decided that she felt the same as he did, it would not be because of any persuasion on his part. She would have to come to him of her own accord. He'd done enough grovelling.

Mollie had turned away to attend to a patient and in that moment it was as if the world held just the two of them. They were close, yet apart, he thought sombrely. In tune rarely, yet in the grip of an attraction that could either take them on a trip to the stars or destroy them.

'Yes,' she said again. 'Why don't we do that? How long have we got?'

'Just two weeks,' he told her, concealing his pleasure. 'Mary's teenage grandaughters are bridesmaids. Jenny from the baker's is putting on a buffet in the church hall, and there'll be a big turnout. Everybody remembers how Frank was trapped under the tractor for hours and how stoic he was. They also admire the way that Toby has been there all the time for him. Just as you have supported *your* father.'

He was giving her the chance to comment, but Giselle just eyed him levelly and turned away. Stop rocking the boat, he told himself, and be grateful that the two of you are talking in the true sense of the word.

'Our shopping trip will have to be this coming Saturday, then,' she said, turning back to face him, and now she was flashing him an impish smile. 'I hope that I might be forgiven for saying that we will need to go into town. I don't see your beloved village being able to supply the kind of clothes we'll need for a wedding.'

He was laughing and Giselle thought how lovely it was to see him back to his usual good humour. She hoped that the children would be just as pleased to be part of the proposed outing in view of their recent reticence.

'I'll allow that,' he agreed. 'We don't have much in the way here of fashion outlets.'

Giselle was still smiling as she remembered how her father had described Raoul's elegant boutique.

When he told the children they were going shopping with Giselle because they'd been invited to a wedding, Alice did a happy little skip around the room and Tom, always more serious, asked, 'Is she not going away, then?'

'I don't know,' Marc told him. 'Maybe, maybe not. But at least Giselle is still here at the moment and is coming with us to Frank and Toby's wedding.'

'Have they chosen you to be the best man because you are better than Mr Fairbank and his son?' Tom asked. 'Why can't they be the best men? It's their weddings.'

'They are the bridegrooms, so they can't be the best men, too,' Marc explained. 'My job as best man will be to take care of the wedding rings until they are ready for them, and make a speech when I toast the bridesmaids.'

'I think you're the "best man" in the whole world,' Alice told him and on that he gave up trying to explain.

'I'll take Saturday morning surgery while you get the children ready,'Giselle had told Marc, and by the time she had seen the last patient of the day the three of them were in Reception, waiting for her.

When she saw them standing there she felt a lump come up in her throat. She was in love with this man, she thought, and loved his children, too, but was that enough to make her want to be the wife of a village doctor with a ready-made family?

It was not what she had planned. Far from it. But today she was going to forget life's complexities and enjoy herself with Marc and his children.

While he was locking up the surgery Giselle and the children got into the car, and when he went to join them he saw that the passenger seat was empty. Giselle was in the back seat, with Alice snuggling up on one side and Tom on the other. He made no comment, just took his place behind the wheel and prayed that the day would continue as it had started.

'So what are the wedding party wearing?' Giselle asked as they approached the outskirts of the town. 'Are you going to have to hire a morning suit?'

He shook his head.

'Frank and Toby aren't really morning suit types. We're all going to be wearing smart dark suits of one kind or another. With regard to the two brides, I believe that Denise has chosen the traditional white wedding dress, complete with veil, and her mother a dress and jacket.'

'I wish I could be a bridesmaid,' Alice said wistfully.

There was silence in the car and Giselle wondered if Marc was thinking that they could perhaps grant Alice *that* wish if they wanted to.

'You *will* be one day,' he told her gently, and with the feeling that it wouldn't be wise to comment further, he left it at that.

'I could do with a new suit,' Marc said as they all trooped into a menswear shop on the high street. He turned to Giselle. 'I thought a navy or black blazer and grey trousers for Tom. What do you think?'

She felt her colour rise. He was making it sound like a family outing, which it was as far as he and the children were concerned, but she was the outsider. The next thing would be the staff in the shop thinking she was his wife.

Each time Marc came out of the cubicle with a different suit on, Giselle was aware of the fresh, wholesome charm of him and her mind went back to when she'd seen him at the auction and had recognised him as the man she'd almost bumped into outside the estate agents.

Even as far back as that she'd felt the pull of his personality. Since then the attraction between them had increased and she wished it hadn't. She wanted to go home and her feelings for Marc were clouding the future.

When he'd chosen a smart navy suit it was a reluctant Tom's turn, with Alice fidgeting on the sidelines, and once the men of the party had gathered up their parcels they all pointed themselves towards the girls' department of a big store.

'Are you all right?' Marc asked in a low voice as he and Giselle followed the children up the escalator.

'Er…yes,' she told him uncertainly, not sure why he'd asked.

'You're not finding us too overpowering?'

'No. But it does feel strange.'

'In what way?'

'I'm not used to this kind of family outings.'

'So you're wishing you hadn't come?'

'No, of course not! I'm only too happy to be of assistance,' she told him, and immediately thought she'd made it sound like a chore instead of a special occasion in her life. So she followed it up quickly with, 'When we've got Alice fixed up with a pretty dress, underwear, shoes, socks and maybe a jacket, as autumn is upon us, it will be my turn to try things on. Then I suggest

222 A FRENCH DOCTOR AT ABBEYFIELDS

that we take the children somewhere for a nice lunch.'

'Agreed, just as long as you realise that the shops here won't come up to those of your beloved Paris, and that Alice and Tom's idea of a nice lunch won't be the same as ours.'

'Of course. The generation gap,' she said, laughing up at him. 'But I think it should be their choice, don't you?'

'Definitely,' he told her, thinking ruefully that *she* was *his* choice, but she didn't want to know it.

They bought Alice a pretty pink dress and all the trappings to go with it, and as Giselle took note of her pleasure she felt tears prick at the thought of her mother. It should be Amanda here with her daughter, she thought, not a stranger who was reluctant to make any commitment to Marc and the children.

On the occasion when she'd gone for Sunday lunch and he'd told her how attracted he was to her, she'd asked him if he'd felt the same way about his wife. Without any hesitation he'd said no, and that he would tell her about Amanda some time. But so far it hadn't happened, as until now they hadn't been communicating.

From the way he'd spoken, she'd gathered that she couldn't use his wife as being too hard an act to follow as an excuse for her reluctance to stay. There'd been disenchantment in his tone and she'd thought that Marc must have felt that his reawakened desires were leading him into more disillusion.

'What colour do you think I should wear?' she asked him when they'd found a shop that suited her tastes.

'Turquoise? Delicate green? Lilac?' he suggested. 'I'd love to see you in cream or pale beige, but I'm told that those are the colours that the older of the two brides has chosen.'

Why couldn't she just choose something without having to consult Marc? she thought. She was behaving like a wife. But he'd asked her to accompany him to the wedding, and even though it was a crazy idea, with their hopes and dreams being so different, she'd thought of nothing else since that day at the surgery when he'd come back from the Fairbank farm in such high spirits.

She didn't want to be too overdressed, especially if Marc's in-laws were going to be there, so she chose a rather staid dress of fine turquoise wool that had never seen a designer label and a matching hat, shoes and handbag.

The outfit was reasonable but far from spellbinding, and when she appeared in it there was silence. Alice's glance held disappointment, and Tom looked down at the carpet outside the changing rooms and scuffed at it with his trainers, which left Marc to be spokesman.

'Are you sure?' he said incredulously. 'I've seen you in far more attractive outfits than that. You'll look like the vicar's wife.'

Angry with herself that she'd made the wrong choice, Giselle snapped back, 'Better that than the doctor's wife!'

'Well, yes,' he said in cold anger. 'Anything would be better than that, wouldn't it? I'm sorry that you don't think a wedding in the village worth dressing up for. Maybe we *are* too uncouth for you.'

The children were listening so, dredging up a smile, she turned to the hovering assistant and told her, 'I'll leave it for now, I think. We can't seem to agree.' After changing back into her own clothes she took Alice by the hand, and swept out of the shop, with Marc and Tom close behind.

Over lunch Giselle put on a front for Tom and Alice's sake. She laughed and chatted with them and Marc did the same, but when her glance met his there was no humour there, no rapport. It had gone with just a few stupid words.

She was regretting her reply when he'd said she would look like the vicar's wife, but was angry at his assumption that she felt herself above the village folk. He had as good as said she was a snob, and it hurt. A fish out of water would be a better description, she thought. But at least now she knew his opinion of her...and Marc would be thinking that he knew her opinion of him when it wasn't true.

Her attempt at dressing down for the wedding instead of up had been her first step towards admitting to herself that she wanted Margaret and Stanley Pollard to approve of her. In the stuffy little cubicle where the idea had come to her there hadn't been time to work out the logic of it. All she'd known had been that she wanted to make Marc happy, and being approved of by his in-laws had seemed like a step in the right direction. In those moments Paris had seemed a million miles away.

When Marc dropped Giselle off at Abbeyfields in the late afternoon she was ready to say she was sorry, but he was looking straight ahead, so she confined her goodbyes to the children and then went disconsolately inside.

She wondered what Marc's reaction would have been if she'd told him that she'd chosen the staid outfit to impress his in-laws. To make them see that she would be a suitable stepmother for their grandchildren. It had been a moment of truth for her, the fact that her thoughts were moving in that direction instead of being filled all the time with the longing to go back to France.

But why couldn't she have just told Marc what was in her mind instead of embarking on the charade of choosing clothes that were not her style? The answer to that question wasn't hard to find. He would have seen it as proof that she'd given in, instead of it being the first uncertain step towards committing herself to a future that she still wasn't sure of. And after today's disagreement, maybe it was just as well that she hadn't.

What had all that been about? Marc was wondering as he carried the packages they'd accumulated into the house. Whatever she wore, Giselle was beautiful to him, and he knew with an aching certainty that without clothes she would be more beautiful still. But there'd been something odd about what had happened at the shop.

When she'd agreed to be his partner at the wedding it had been like the sun coming out from behind the clouds after those weeks of no communication, and he'd envisaged her looking stunning in whatever she chose to wear, but instead…

His comment about the vicar's wife and the answer she'd flung back at him had sent the day onto a downward slope. Now there was nothing left to do but get through the rest of the weekend and hope that Giselle didn't change her mind about going to the wedding with him.

'Can we go round to Grandma and Grandad's to show them our new clothes?' Alice asked.

'Er, yes, why not?' he said. It would be something to fill the empty evening.

Marc wasn't the only one who saw the weekend stretching ahead emptily. When they'd cleared away after their evening meal and her father had settled in front of the television, Giselle decided to go for a walk.

It was chilly outside and darkness had fallen, but when she reached the centre of the village there was a lot of activity around The Peaks, the popular public house. With a sudden yearning for light, warmth and the company of others, she went in, ordered a drink at the bar and then looked around her.

There were a lot of teenagers inside, bent on enjoying Saturday night, and amongst them a smattering of adults. She didn't know anyone there and thought that it was comforting to be amongst strangers. It was a pleasure to be ignored instead of the object of everyone's interest, until she heard a familiar voice coming from somewhere out of sight.

When she peered into a small alcove nearby Marc was there, seated at a table with a group of a similar age to himself. When he saw her his jaw went slack with surprise, then he was on his feet and coming towards her. So much for being amongst strangers, she thought, and so much for her visions of Marc having a miserable evening, too.

'What are *you* doing here?' he asked in a low voice.

'I went for a walk, but it was chilly outside,' she told him. 'So I came in here instead. I thought it might help to dispel the image of the vicar's wife.'

'I shouldn't have said that,' he commented wryly. 'Deidre is a lovely woman and has been known to call in here for a half of Guinness when the mood takes her. It was just that I'm so used to you looking stunning that you took me by surprise. I'd had visions of you putting all the other women in the shade at the wedding.'

'Even the two brides? I think not. And who's being the snob now?' she countered. 'Where are the children?'

'Staying the night with Margaret and Stan. Alice wanted to show her grandparents the new clothes we'd bought for the wedding and they asked them if they wanted to stop over.'

'What did they have to say about Alice's dress?'

'They could see that you'd had a hand in choosing it.'

'And?'

'They thought it was lovely.'

Giselle took a deep breath. 'Did they have any objections to me being part of the shopping trip?'

'Not that I was aware of. They are both realists. Though I imagine they would rather I spent my time with someone local, instead of the elegant French butterfly who has fluttered into our midst. There must be the fear in them that they would lose touch with the children if I married someone who wasn't local and went to live somewhere else.'

'It would be wrong if that happened,' Giselle commented.

'What? Me marrying someone who isn't local? Or going to live somewhere else?'

'Both of those things, *and* their grandparents losing touch with the children. Your place is here.'

He took her hand and led her out into the cool

autumn night. In the darkness of the deserted beer garden he turned her round to face him.

'Do I detect another sidetracking manoeuvre? Are you using Amanda's parents as an excuse to keep us apart? Because you're wrong when you state so firmly that my place is here. My place is where *you* are—*you* and the children—and wherever it might be, I would never let the bond between them and their grandparents be severed.'

She had gone weak at the knees. Marc was telling her that he would be prepared to pull up his roots and leave this place that he loved so much for her, which should have made it easier for her to make a decision. But it didn't. She would feel guilty for ever if she let him do that.

There was loud music coming from the pub and she said, 'Can we get away from this place?'

'Yes,' he said. 'I'll walk you home.'

As they walked the short distance to Abbeyfields she said in a low voice, 'Real love consists of giving and taking equally. If

I'm the woman we're discussing, I couldn't let you do what you're suggesting. *You* would be giving up everything and I nothing.'

'What about your freedom?' he asked. 'Giving it up to take on a ready-made family. But none of this matters unless you love me. *Do* you love me, Giselle?'

Of course she loved him, she thought painfully. Would they be having this discussion if she didn't? But *she* wasn't as generous as he when it came to settling down in a strange land. Her father had done it, Marc was willing to, but she was her own person.

'I think of you all the time, if that's anything to go by,' she told him in answer to his question, and watched his expression tighten.

'For goodness' sake! I've known people to have someone on their mind all the time because they hate them. When I kissed you that one and only time, you melted in my arms. It was as if we were meant for each other, but ever since then our relationship has been up and down like a yo-yo.'

He stopped suddenly beneath the light of a streetlamp and, reaching out for her, said, 'Maybe it's time we saw some action instead of the everlasting battle of words.'

Before she could reply she was in his arms with his mouth on hers, and nothing else mattered.

When at last they drew apart Marc murmured against the soft swathe of her hair, 'I usually have one or the other or both of the children creeping into my bed at some time in the night. But as they're sleeping over with their grandparents, there's going to be lots of space. So would you consider—?'

He didn't get the chance to finish what he was saying. A voice from behind was calling his name urgently, and when they swivelled round they saw the landlord of The Peaks running towards them.

'What's wrong, Bob?' Marc asked.

'A youngster has just collapsed in the pub,' he said breathlessly. 'He's having some kind of fit. I'd seen you both in there and thought I might catch you. Will you come and have a look at him? I've sent for an ambulance.'

'Yes, of course,' Marc said immediately, and with Giselle beside him they rushed back to where a group of teenagers was crowded round one of their number who was lying on the floor. He was writhing and jerking uncontrollably as the two doctors arrived on the scene.

'It's Damien!' Marc exclaimed as they hurried across to him. 'He's the son of friends of mine who are on holiday abroad at the moment.'

'And is he epileptic?' Giselle asked as they bent over him.

'Not that I know of,' he replied. 'He's never consulted me about anything like that.'

'He has the symptoms, Marc. Froth on the lips and convulsions.'

'Yes, but, like I say, I have no knowledge of him having epilepsy.' He turned to the other members of the group and asked, 'Did any of you see Damien take anything before this happened?'

'I did,' one of the girls piped up. 'I saw him

take a pill and asked him what it was, and he said to mind my own business.'

'See if the ambulance is coming, Bob,' Marc told the hovering landlord. He turned to Giselle, who was feeling the lad's pulse. 'Let's put my jacket beneath his head and make him as comfortable as possible. That's about all we can do for him until the emergency services arrive.

'To my knowledge, Darren hasn't got epilepsy,' he repeated firmly, 'but there always has to be that first seizure, I suppose. Alternatively, if he's taken something he shouldn't have, *that* could have brought on the attack and it will be stomach-pump time.'

'His pulse is fast,' Giselle told him, 'and if it is epilepsy, he should be coming round by now.'

'We were fooling about on the village green before we came in here,' another youth said awkwardly.

'What do you mean by fooling about?' Marc asked.

'You know...wrestling...and throwing each other.'

'Really?' he said dryly, adding to Giselle, 'So it could be from a blow to the head, a tablet of some sort or the onset of epilepsy. If his parents were here, they would be going ballistic, but it's no use worrying about that at the moment. I'm going to go with him to the hospital in the absence of any relatives and see what surfaces.'

He flashed her a wry grin. 'To think that I almost had you in my clutches. That big bed of mine isn't going to have *anyone* sleeping in it tonight the way things are going.'

The ambulance was pulling up outside. She could hear its tyres grinding to a halt and within minutes the paramedics had stretchered Damien aboard and Marc had climbed in beside him.

As Giselle walked home she was thinking that if Damien hadn't been taken ill she would have spent the night in Marc's arms. There was nothing surer than that after what had happened between them earlier, and once they'd made love the decision would have been made for her.

Yet she didn't want it to be like that, giving in to the attraction between them because they'd slept together. She wanted her decision to be made in the cold light of day, logically, calmly, without the demands of the senses being involved. So maybe the fates had stepped in when least expected.

CHAPTER NINE

GISELLE rang Marc early on Sunday morning, not sure if he would be back from the hospital but keen to know how their young patient was progressing.

There was no reply and her anxiety remained unrelieved. She rang him again half an hour later and he was there, sounding somewhat weary but his usual organised self when it came to the sick and suffering.

'I've only just got back,' he told her. 'The convulsions had subsided by the time we got to the hospital, but young Damien was scared stiff about what had happened to him, as we all are when our bodies go out of control, so I stayed with him through the night.

'He was missing his mum and dad, of

course, but fortunately they're due back today. It's the first time they've left him on his own, so when they discover what's happened it will rather take the edge off the holiday, I'm afraid.'

'Are we any nearer to knowing what caused the fit?' Giselle asked.

'Yes and no. The tablet that someone saw him take wasn't anything suspicious. He'd banged his head earlier in the afternoon when there'd been horseplay between some of the lads, and it was a painkiller that he'd taken. I don't mind telling you I sent up a prayer of thanks when I heard that.'

'So what was it, then? Not damage to the skull from what he'd been up to in the afternoon, I hope?'

'No. He's been X-rayed and had a scan so it *is* beginning to look as if it might be the onset of epilepsy. They'll be doing tests today and giving him an ECG. But there won't be anything to indicate if the fit was just an isolated incident or if it will happen again. As we both know, there are divided opinions in the medical profession as to whether a patient should be put on anticonvulsant drugs after just the one seizure. So for young Damien it's wait-and-see time.'

'Do his parents know yet?' asked Giselle.

'I've popped a note through their letterbox, asking them to ring me as soon as they get in,' replied Marc. 'I wouldn't want them to hear what's happened from another source, knowing the village grapevine.'

There was a pause. 'And what about us, Giselle!' he said, his voice deepening with regret. 'We had the chance to be together and no sooner had it been given to us than it was taken away.'

'Yes, I know,' she said slowly, 'but maybe it was meant to be.'

There was a long moment of silence and she could feel her palms becoming moist as she gripped the phone.

'Meant to be?' he echoed in angry incredulity. 'So you aren't sorry that we didn't make love? You saw Damien's sudden illness as fortuitous? I suppose it was the escape route that you're always on the lookout for. Even after I'd just told you I would move to be with you! It would seem even *that* isn't enough. So I can only conclude that *I'm* the problem. The pushy guy who keeps trying to make you fall in love with him.'

As she opened her mouth to protest he went on inexorably, 'Well, I have news for you, Giselle. I am finally prepared to admit that it won't work. You are right about one thing, you *don't* belong here. You have finally convinced me. I've offered to move to wherever *you* want to be, but you're still playing hard to get so there is nothing else to say. Except that I'm sorry the thought of us making love appealed to you so little.'

When he paused for breath she was ready to say her piece but the line had gone dead, and as she stood looking down at the receiver the finality of it all hit her.

But anger was stirring now. She'd been going to tell him that never, ever would she let him leave the village. If *she* didn't belong here, *he* certainly did. So did his children.

It wasn't Marc who was the problem. She was. Or had been until the previous day when she'd taken the first step towards making the decision that would change her life, by wanting his in-laws to approve of her.

But he'd just made it clear that he'd had enough. He'd jumped to conclusions and couldn't believe that she had wanted him as much as he'd wanted her after they'd been in each other's arms on the way home to Abbeyfields.

Of course she couldn't blame Marc for thinking she was blowing hot and cold all the time. But all that had changed. If he'd given her the chance she'd have told him that she felt the same as he did. That where *he* was, *she* had to be also. Even if it meant staying in this Cheshire village that was slowly casting its spell over her.

It was just a week to the Fairbank wedding and she knew how much Marc and the rest of the villagers were looking forward to it. She would do nothing until it was over, she decided. Then she would go to Paris to say her goodbyes.

He couldn't believe it, Marc thought bleakly when he'd put the phone down. As he'd watched over Damien in a cubicle in Accident and Emergency there'd been an aching disappointment inside him because he'd hoped that he and Giselle were going to spend the night together, and some time during those enchanted hours he would have asked her to marry him.

When he went to collect the children his father-in-law said, 'You look somewhat bleary-eyed. What have you been up to?'

'I spent the night in hospital, sitting beside one of our local teenagers,' he told him dryly.

Stanley didn't miss the tone and he hid a smile. 'Am I to take it that you would rather have been keeping someone else company? Such as the glamorous doctor who has replaced me at the surgery for the time being?'

'For the time being' was a good description

of Giselle's place in his life, Marc thought flatly, but he had to smile at Stanley's astuteness. The old guy was obviously feeling better.

He hadn't met Giselle, but Margaret would have reported back on her, and as if to confirm it he went on to say, 'You do know that Margaret and I would like to see you marry again, don't you? Though we had hoped it might be someone we knew. But obviously the choice is yours, Marc.'

The elderly GP turned away and looked sombrely out of the window, and when he spoke again Marc's face went blank with surprise. 'I've never said this before to a soul, not even her mother, but I feel you had a raw deal with Amanda. She was a spoilt madam and selfish with it. Don't make the same mistake again.'

Marc took a deep breath. 'I *am* in love with Giselle Howard,' he told his father-in-law, 'and I think she cares for me, but she cares for Paris more. I get the impression that she feels stifled here in the Cheshire countryside, and remember I don't come empty-handed. I have Tom and Alice.'

'If she really loves you, none of that will matter,' Stanley told him. 'You're taking her to the Fairbank wedding, aren't you? So that's a step in the right direction.'

'I was, but strong words have passed between us. Or maybe I should say that I've said strong words and Giselle has had to listen. So whether she will want anything to do with me in the future is in the balance.'

'In other words, you've given up on her. That doesn't sound like you.'

'I know, but there is a limit to how long I can stand being around Giselle in such uncertainty.'

During the week that followed there was a serenity about Giselle that made Marc want to shake her. While he was feeling restless and on edge, she was behaving as if he'd never said those angry words to her over the phone and he found it irritating. A few times he caught her smiling a secret little smile and it irked him even more, but there was no way he wanted any more confrontations.

He sensed that her tranquillity was connected with him telling her that this thing between them was over. Though 'over' was hardly the right way to describe it. For something to be over, it had to begin. But Giselle was obviously happy now that he'd given up on her.

With regard to himself, he was going through the motions of daily living as best he could, telling himself that asking Giselle to join the practice had not been a good idea. It might have been if she'd felt the same way he did—together they would have been fantastic.

Sometimes he wished that she would just go and put an end to it, but she'd already said a few times that she wasn't going anywhere until she was sure that her father would be all right without her. What he, Marc, would be like without her didn't seem to concern her.

The only thing he'd said to her of a personal nature in recent days had been to ask if she was still going to the wedding with him and she'd said, yes, she was, if he had no objections.

He was hardly likely to object as this would probably be the last time they were ever together outside surgery hours.

'No, I've no objections,' he'd told her unsmilingly. 'The ceremony is at twelve, so I'll see you at the church. I can't call for you as I'll need to be at the farm, performing my best man's duties, such as sorting out the rings, all four of them, and calming down the bridegrooms, all two of them.'

'What about Alice and Tom?' she'd asked. 'Are they going with their grandparents?'

'Well, yes, they'll have to,' he'd said dryly, 'as I'll be otherwise engaged and there's no one else to take them.'

He'd put out a feeler to see if Giselle would offer. She would have done a week ago, but there was no such suggestion forthcoming now and he left it at that. He knew that as far as he was concerned, all the pleasurable anticipation had gone, but there was no way that

Frank and Toby were going to know that. It would be their day and he would be there for them every step of the way.

'Would you be all right without me for a few days?' Giselle asked her father the morning after Marc had said he'd given up on her.

He observed her in surprise.

Yes, of course I will. I'm feeling better than I've felt in ages. Where are you thinking of going?'

'I haven't decided. I need to get my thoughts in order and to do that I have to be away from Marc for a few days.'

'So it's like that, is it?' he'd said, and she'd nodded.

'Yes, it's like that.'

It had been all she'd said and her father hadn't questioned her further, but she knew he was concerned about her. She also knew that he was someone else who would like her to stay in the village, but he would never try to influence her in any way.

* * *

On the morning of the wedding Giselle dressed with great care. There hadn't really been any need for her to go shopping for clothes that day when she'd gone with Marc and the children. She'd pretended that there had been so that she wouldn't be the odd one out, with not very good results. Her mouth curved into a smile at the memory of Marc's dismay when she'd come prancing out of the cubicle in the staid outfit and he'd admitted that he'd been expecting her to look stunning instead of a replica of the vicar's wife.

It would serve him right if Deidre turned up with a bare midriff in a see-through designer outfit, she thought whimsically as she took her own choice out of the wardrobe. It was a plain, understated yet very elegant dress of pale green silk. With a wide-brimmed hat of the same colour and gold bag and shoes to match, it made the pale olive of her skin glow and brought out the highlights in the dark brown swathe of her hair, which she'd taken up off her face into a soft coronet.

What would Marc think when he saw this? she wondered. Probably that she was deliberately mocking him. Dressing how he'd wanted her to now that he'd given up on her.

The church was full to overflowing when she got there, but a young usher, who Giselle recognised as Damien, showed her to an empty pew in the second row from the front.

She had no sooner seated herself than there was a scuffle from behind and Alice and Tom appeared beside her, resplendent in the clothes they'd bought on the shopping trip.

'Can we sit with you, Giselle?' Alice whispered.

'Yes, of course,' she said as pleasure washed over her. 'But where are your grandma and grandad?'

'Just behind us,' Tom said, and when she turned to check if it was all right with them, she received a smiling nod from Margaret, which made her wonder if it was because Marc had told her there was nothing between them, or if she'd been vetted and had passed the test.

'You both look fantastic,' she told the children.

They preened themselves and Alice whispered, 'So do you.' Then added with sudden childish anxiety, 'I hope that Daddy is all right.'

'Why do you say that?' she asked.

'He was poorly last night. We had to keep giving him drinks and paracetamol because he was hurting so much. Tom thought we should ring you as you're our friend *and* a doctor, but Daddy said, no, definitely not.'

Well, he would, wouldn't he? she thought, and wondered how long she could last without making things right between the two of them. But Marc ill? How was he now? she wondered, looking down at his two young carers.

'And so how was he this morning?' she asked.

'Still poorly…and sad,' Tom said. 'Daddy is always sad since you don't come to see us anymore.'

Giselle sighed. Marc would not have been

happy if he'd heard that, she thought, but there were more important things to be concerned about. He was ill and she needed to know what was wrong. Obviously he wasn't so bad that he'd had to miss the wedding, and as any moment he and the two bridegrooms would be arriving, she would be able to see for herself how ill he was.

When she looked up he was there, approaching from a side entrance of the church with Frank and Toby. She saw immediately that the children hadn't exaggerated. He looked pale and drawn, nothing like his usual self.

Yet he was in control, smiling across at the packed pews and with a special twinkly smile for Tom and Alice, but it faded when his glance rested on her, Giselle noticed. There was a different expression on his face now and she recognised it as sardonic irony. He'd no doubt noticed what she was wearing and was remembering her first choice.

But she didn't care about that. He was ill and she loved him. It was typical of him that he'd thrown it off for Frank and Toby's sake when probably all he'd wanted to do was stay in bed.

The organ had struck up the wedding march. The brides had arrived and everyone rose to their feet. Mother and daughter were smiling as they walked down the aisle together, having decided to give each other away, and behind them were the bridesmaids, revelling in their moment of glory.

When they drew level Giselle gave Alice's hand a squeeze and whispered, 'One day it will be your turn.'

'Yes,' Alice whispered back. 'I can't wait.'

Maybe you won't have to, Giselle thought, and switched her glance back to Marc.

As the two couples made their vows Giselle's heartbeat was quickening. These were good people, she thought. They hadn't known each other long—like Marc and herself—but there must have been an instant rapport between them, too. The only difference was that none of them had been beset by yearnings to go back to where they'd come from, like she had.

It had taken a very special man to make her see where her real future lay and soon, if he hadn't shut her out of his life for ever, she would tell him what he wanted to hear.

But first she had to find out what was wrong with him and deal with it. In their job they could easily pick up something from a patient. The moment she got the chance to talk to him she would be asking questions from a doctor's point of view.

Marc had almost finished his best man's duties. He'd just made his speech and presented the little bridesmaids with pretty bracelets. Soon the two happy couples would go back to the farm to start their married lives, as a honeymoon was not possible with the animals to look after and the crops to see to. When the guests started to drift away, she would be able to talk to Marc.

He still looked awful and her anxiety was increasing by the minute, but each time she tried to get him on his own someone required his presence and she sensed that he was only too pleased to be called away.

But at last the village hall was empty. Jenny and her helpers from the bakery had cleared away what was left of the buffet and it was time to go, but not before she'd spoken to him.

'What's wrong?' she asked as they went out to their cars. 'The children said you'd been ill in the night and you look pretty dreadful now.'

'I don't know,' he said abruptly. 'I've probably picked up some sort of bug, but I don't care as long as I haven't let Frank and Toby down.'

'*You* haven't let anybody down,' she told him patiently. 'You never do, but can we please get you somewhere where I can examine you?'

'I'm all right,' he protested. 'Where are the children?'

'Gone with their grandparents. They're going to bring them round later so that you can go to bed for a while.'

He had his car keys in his hand and before he could argue further Giselle took them from him and dropped them into her handbag.

'I know that you don't want me around,' she told him, 'but that's too bad. I'm taking you home and I'm staying there until I've sorted out what is wrong with you.'

He was paler than ever and without giving him the chance to argue further she opened the passenger door of her car and waited for him to get in.

'It's appendicitis,' he said as he slumped down in the seat. 'Just take me to the hospital, Giselle.'

'Appendicitis!' she gasped. 'But you're not in any pain.'

'I was during the night, but it's eased off, which means that...'

As his voice trailed away she interrupted frantically. 'It means that it might burst! How could you take such a risk?'

'I couldn't miss the wedding,'

'Of course you could,' she cried, flinging herself into the driver's seat. 'A perforated appendix can be very serious. You're a doctor, for heaven's sake!'

'I'm not stupid,' he said wearily. 'I've been monitoring myself. I should be all right if we don't waste any time.'

'And were you intending driving yourself to the hospital?' she asked stonily.

'We are talking about a ten-minute drive.'

'We are also talking about an appendix that might burst at any time,' she said tightly, and after that there was silence in the car.

When Marc had been examined in A and E the consultant, who was someone he knew, said, 'You've cut this a bit fine, boyo. Haven't got a death wish, have you? We'd better get you up to Theatre pronto.' He turned to Giselle. 'Are you Marc's wife?'

'No. I'm not his wife,' she told him as they waited for the porter to take Marc to the operating theatre. 'I'm just a colleague who works at the practice with him.'

'So why did you let him take such a risk? It's a miracle the appendix hasn't burst. He must have been in agony before it got to this stage.'

'Yes, he was,' she agreed. 'That was during the night,'

'So why…?'

'He was best man at a wedding today and wouldn't let the wedding party down,' she called over her shoulder as she hurried alongside the trolley, which the porter was wheeling towards the operating theatre.

If Marc had heard their conversation he didn't say anything. He was lying on the trolley looking limp and ashen and the fear that had never left her since he'd informed her of his self-diagnosis increased.

Supposing he died still thinking that she didn't want him, that she was the cold snob he'd accused her of being, she kept thinking as the minutes ticked slowly by.

At last a face appeared out of the mists of her misery and it was smiling.

'Marc is in Recovery,' she was told. 'He was right about the appendix and took some degree of risk, but he knew what he was doing. Most of us have met him at some time or another and we all know he's a man of his word. If he'd promised to be somebody's best man he would move heaven and earth to keep his promise.'

As she sat beside him in a dimly lit side ward later that night, Giselle was thinking that Marc was known to be a man of his word, was he? So would he change his mind about her? She'd thought that there would be no more complications once she'd said her goodbyes to Paris, but maybe the rift had gone too far for that.

She'd phoned Margaret and Stanley and they'd been dumbfounded to hear that Marc had been operated on for appendicitis. 'Obviously we'll keep Alice and Tom here,' Margaret had said, 'and one of us will bring them to see him first thing in the morning.'

'I'll have gone by then,' Giselle had told her. 'I'll need to spend the day at the surgery, preparing for Monday morning without him, but I'll be in touch.'

'We'd be glad of that,' she'd said. 'And, Giselle…'

'Yes?' Giselle had questioned warily.

'I'm sorry I wasn't more affable that day at the surgery. You were a stranger. I should have made you more welcome. Maybe you'll come round to have a meal with us some time, so that we can get to know you.'

'I'd love to,' she'd told the older woman, before going back to sit by Marc.

When he regained consciousness Marc could smell Giselle's perfume but he couldn't see her, and then as everything became clearer she was there, standing by the window, looking out into the dark night, still dressed in the clothes she'd worn for the wedding and not aware that he was awake.

'I liked the outfit,' he said drowsily, and she turned and was by his side instantly.

'How are you feeling?' she asked softly.

He sighed.

'Sore. I could have done without this, with the children to care for and the practice to run.'

She smiled down at him.

'Just because we're doctors, it doesn't mean that we don't get sick. The worst is over. You'll soon be back on your feet.'

'And in the meantime?' he questioned grimly.

'In the meantime I'll keep the practice running, along with Craig and the rest of your faithful staff, and your in-laws and I will take care of the children. They're bringing Alice and Tom to see you in the morning.'

He nodded, his anxieties momentarily appeased.

'Don't let Frank and Toby know that I was suffering while the wedding was on, will you? Let them think that it came on suddenly when it was all over, otherwise it will be a cloud on their day and I don't want that.'

'Anything to make you happy,' she told him.

'*Anything?* I don't think so,' he said flatly, 'but that's all in the past. We all take the wrong turning at times.'

'Yes, don't we?' Giselle agreed, not to be drawn.

A nurse approached and said, 'The consultant will be along shortly to see Dr Bannerman and we'd like him to get some rest until then.'

'Yes, of course,' Giselle said. Planting a butterfly kiss on his brow, she left him, with a promise to come back later.

She'd phoned her father to explain what had happened and when she got home in a cool autumn dawn he was having an early breakfast.

'How is Marc?' were his first words. 'There never seems to be a dull moment where the two of you are concerned.'

'I wouldn't argue about that,' she told him tiredly. 'He'd been officiating at the wedding with an appendix ready to burst. Fortunately it didn't and he's now recovering. It is going to be a busy time for me and his in-laws while he's recuperating.'

'So it's goodbye to the break that you'd promised yourself.'

'Yes, for the time being. For now I'm going to get out of my clothes, have a shower, followed by some breakfast, then I'm going to the surgery to get organised for tomorrow without Marc.'

'There'll be some upset in the village when they hear about this,' he commented.

'What? Me in charge of the surgery?' she asked with a smile.

'No. The doctor that they all trust and like being out of action. Though it could be worse. They're only deprived of him temporarily. It's not as if he's leaving the place.'

Was that a word of caution for her? Giselle wondered as she stripped off the clothes that she'd been wearing for what seemed like a lifetime.

CHAPTER TEN

MARC was discharged from the hospital after a few days.

He would have been back at the practice the next day if he hadn't been faced with the united front of Giselle, Craig and all the rest of the staff, who flatly refused to let him lift a finger for at least another two weeks.

The children had stayed with their grandparents while he'd been in hospital, but soon they would be back home and Marc was hoping that then life would be a step nearer to normality.

Now that he was well on the way to recovery, he wasn't seeing much of Giselle, but he told himself wryly that he hadn't been seeing much of her before. Apart from the time when he'd come round in the hospital he'd only seen her for brief moments, which he understood with the weight of the practice on her shoulders. Yet it niggled.

But the rest of those who knew him had made up for it. He'd been inundated with visitors while he'd been in hospital, including the two newlywed couples, who fortunately had no idea of how ill he'd felt at the wedding.

He'd also had a visit from Damien and his parents. The youngster *had* been diagnosed as having had an epileptic seizure, but the family was keeping their fingers crossed as he hadn't had any since and hadn't yet been prescribed anti-convulsant drugs.

Irene, the woman with Munchausen's syndrome, had called in, too. Glad of the opportunity to be on hospital premises, she had observed him enviously as he lay in bed.

In fact, half the village had appeared by his bedside, but rarely Giselle. Yet what could he expect? he'd asked himself. He had given her her marching orders so she wasn't likely to be falling over herself to be with him.

On his first night home he'd thought thankfully that he could see her whenever he wanted now. She was within easy reach and soon he would be back in the surgery with her there all the time, which was strange sort of thinking for the man who'd told her he'd finished with her and she didn't belong in the village.

No one had actually put it into words but he sensed that Giselle had passed the test with Margaret and Stanley, which was ironic now that it was too late. He supposed it was some slight comfort to know that if anything had come of his love for her, he wouldn't have had *that* problem to overcome.

In those first days back home it felt strange to be able to do the household chores in a leisurely manner instead of trying to fit them in when possible. The morning rush to get the children to school was now a leisurely exercise while he had time on his hands, but when the day arrived for him to return to the practice he was good and ready for two reasons. He loved the job…and he loved Giselle.

* * *

When Marc pulled up in front of the surgery that first morning he had to laugh. There was a banner above the doorway that said WELCOME BACK DR BANNERMAN. WE HAVE MISSED YOU.

And I've missed you, he thought. One of you in particular.

It was so good to be back, he thought when he went out to his car at the end of morning surgery. Being away from there and the village in general had been like cutting off his life's blood. The only thing taking the edge off his contentment was the atmosphere between himself and Giselle. She'd never referred to the harsh words that he'd said that night on the phone, so he had to conclude that his opinions were of so little interest to her that she couldn't be bothered to take him up on them.

The serenity she'd displayed the week before the wedding was still there, as if she had risen above petty wrangles, and he had a sinking feeling that he knew why. She was going back to Paris. How soon and when he would have to wait to find out.

As he was getting into his car Toby came trundling along the street on one of the farm's tractors, and when he saw Marc he stopped.

'Morning, Doctor,' he said. 'How are you feeling?'

'I'm fine, Toby,' Marc told him. 'How are you?'

'On top of the world. Couldn't be better. We was wondering if your young 'uns would like a piglet, or a young goat, or both if you've got the space, to say thanks for being our best man.'

'Er…it's nice of you to offer,' he said, taken aback. 'But I'm not sure that my back garden is suitable for such things.'

'They could keep them at Abbeyfields,' Giselle's voice said from behind him. 'My father would help look after them.'

'There you are, then,' Toby said. 'Bring the youngsters round and they can choose their own.'

He bent down from his high seat on the tractor and said in a low voice, 'Talking about young 'uns, my missus has missed. She'll be coming to see you soon, Dr Howard. You can see why I'm over the moon, can't you?'

When he'd gone Marc said, 'You didn't have to do that. You're binding the children to you with gentle bonds, but you won't be around when they're upset and missing you.'

'For goodness' sake, Marc,' she protested. 'Whatever I choose to do, my father isn't going anywhere. Nothing is going to stop Tom and Alice from going to Abbeyfields for as long as they want, so will you please stop finding fault with me?' Leaving him feeling that the brightness had suddenly gone from the morning, she drove off towards the hill road and the first of her home visits.

It was incredible, Marc thought as he followed her some minutes later.

He never got it right with Giselle. Whereas Toby, who only a couple of months ago had had nothing going for him other than hard graft at the farm, was now married and already joyfully facing the possibility of parenthood. While he himself had made the mistake of falling in love with someone who didn't want him.

To say that the children were delighted with the offer from the Fairbanks would be an understatement. Alice had insisted that Giselle go with them to choose the animals and Marc had gone along with it, telling himself that it would be another memory to look back on as the empty years went by.

As they drove home with the animals in a trailer behind Marc's car and a list of instructions regarding their feeding and general care, Tom said, 'We've decided that we're going to call the goat Geronimo and the piglet...'

'Princess Pinky,' Alice chimed in.

'Clever thinking,' Marc said solemnly. Giselle hid a smile.

She was happy, happy to be with him and the children, and if he wasn't feeling the same, she hoped he soon would, but she had to do it her way. Close one chapter of her life before another opened.

Two weeks later Giselle said to him, 'I'd like to take a few days off now that you are well again. It's been stressful without you and I'd like to get away for a change of scene.'

'Yes, of course,' Marc said stiffly, aware of how much he would have liked to be included in whatever she was planning. 'Is your father going with you?'

'Er…no. I'm going alone,' she said quickly, and he thought she'd wanted to get that in before he had the chance to ask if she was going with someone else, like the fellow in the expensive suit for instance, though they'd seen nothing of him since that one appearance.

But were those warning bells that were clanging in his mind? he asked himself. Could this be it? Had she waited until he was back in harness before departing?

It might be. Her father looked fit enough

these days. Maybe he should ask him to come in for a check-up. It would help him to be prepared for the knock-out blow when it came, as there was no way he was going to start interfering if that *was* what she was planning.

'So when do you want to be off?' he asked abruptly.

'From this Thursday,' she replied.

'Until when?'

'I'm not sure. Can we leave it open?'

'Yes, if you want,' he agreed reluctantly, with a growing feeling that he was right. This was the moment he'd been dreading.

When she'd gone back into her own room he stood deep in thought. The simple thing would be to ask her father what plans Giselle was making, but he couldn't do that, check up on her on the sly. And if her father didn't want to answer his questions because she had told him not to, it would put Philip in an awkward position.

'Did you see anything of Giselle while I was in hospital?' Marc asked the children that evening. He didn't know why he was asking but he had to have something to hold on to.

'Yes,' Alice piped up. 'She came to see us every day, and once she minded us when Grandma and Grandad had to go somewhere.'

Really! he thought, and wondered why no one had bothered to tell him. He was grateful in one way, yet not in another. How could she want to strengthen the bond between them and herself and yet be unwilling to relieve *his* misery?

On the Wednesday night he lay sleepless for hours. One moment he thought he should go and face Giselle. Bring it all out into the open, his feelings, her plans. And the next he was telling himself that he'd said his piece the morning after she'd let slip that she was relieved they hadn't slept together. Why should anything be different now?

When he'd come out of the pit of unconsciousness in the hospital and had found her there with him, his heart had rejoiced. She'd been kind and loving towards him and he'd been prepared to take back all he'd said, but in the days that had followed he'd seen so little of her he'd had to accept that nothing had changed. Giselle was still the enigma that she'd been from the start.

As she prepared for the trip to Paris Giselle was calmer than she'd been in months She'd made her decision and now it was time to let go. She had made a last-minute booking for the flight, but first thing Thursday morning the tickets were on the mat when she got up. And by a strange coincidence with them were brochures for apartments in Paris from a firm who dealt with properties for sale there. She'd registered with them when she'd first come to England, so that when she was ready to go back she would be informed on locations and prices. She didn't need them now but scooped them into her bag with the tickets rather than leave them around.

Her father knew she was going away and when he'd asked where, she'd been evasive, telling him that she was just going to set off and see where her feet took her. If she were to tell him she was going to Paris he might mention it to Marc and she didn't want that to happen.

He'd accepted what he'd been told and wouldn't have thought twice about it if he hadn't been down before her and seen the flight tickets and the brochures amongst the post.

He said nothing when she came down but his mind had been going round in circles as he recalled how the other day Giselle had said, 'You'll be all right on your own, won't you? I'll phone as soon as I arrive wherever I'm going.'

It wasn't like her to be secretive, Philip thought. It had to have something to do with Marc, he was sure of it, but what? *He* would welcome him as a son-in-law, but did Giselle want him as a husband? he wondered. Maybe his daughter was too bogged down with the past.

He watched Giselle drive off and then went to get his coat. If he was making a mistake, he could only tell her he was sorry when she came back, but he couldn't just stand by and watch without doing something.

The waiting room at the surgery was almost empty and Philip breathed a sigh of relief. 'Could I have a quick word with Dr Bannerman?' he asked one of the reception-ists, and when she hesitated he told her, 'It is extremely urgent. A personal matter.'

She nodded.

'All right. As soon as the patient who is with him comes out, you can go in.'

'Mr Howard!' Marc exclaimed. He looked down at the pile of patients' records on his desk and said, 'I don't seem to have your notes here. Do you have an appointment?'

'No,' Philip said hurriedly. 'I'm quite well. Although you might think I need my head examined when I tell you why I'm here. It's about Giselle.'

Marc had been leaning back in his chair, ob-serving his unexpected visitor, but that brought him upright. 'What about Giselle?'

'She's flying to Paris this morning, Marc,' he told him. 'Flight tickets came in the post, and because she hadn't wanted to tell me where she was going I took a peep. There were brochures on properties in the same post and I thought you should be told.'

'So you know that I'm in love with her?'

'Yes. I guessed.'

Marc was on his feet even as they were speaking. 'I don't know whether you've done me a favour or not,' he told him, 'but you have my grateful thanks.' Before Philip could reply he'd gone, grabbing his coat off a hook behind him as he went.

As Giselle approached the checkout desk at the airport she was smiling. For the first time in months she could see the way ahead. Losing her mother and moving to England so quickly afterwards had left her grieving and lost. Then she'd met a man above all men, kind, caring, passionate…and impatient.

She'd left two loves behind when she'd left

France, the mother she had adored and the beautiful city where she'd been brought up, and though from the moment of meeting she'd been attracted to Marc, she'd needed time before admitting how much she cared for him. But now she was ready to do so. In two days' time she would be back, ready to share her life with him if he still wanted her.

When she turned away from the checkout desk, her eyes widened. A man, broad-shouldered, blue-eyed, with a pelt of thick fair hair was striding purposefully towards her through the airport crowd, and there was something in his expression that told her he wasn't there for plane spotting!

Giselle was smiling when he reached her, while Marc felt as if he would choke with disappointment. 'How could you?' he said through gritted teeth. 'You were going without a word of farewell, weren't you? If you didn't want to say goodbye to *me,* you could at least have told Tom and Alice and the staff at the practice that you weren't going to be around any more. And what about your father? Are you just leaving him high and dry in that big house?'

Giselle had the folder that held the tickets in her hand, and incredibly she was still smiling as she said softly, 'I don't know who told you I would be here, but I can make a guess. Do you see this, Marc?' She placed an airline ticket in his hand and he looked down at it blankly. 'It's a return ticket to Paris from Manchester. I'm going there to do two things—visit my mother's grave and say goodbye to the city I was brought up in. Then I'm coming back because I love you, Marc. I love your children…and I love your village.'

'I don't believe it,' he breathed. 'I thought you'd gone without a word and left me in despair for the rest of my life.'

'So will you be here waiting for me when I get back?' she asked.

'Will I be here? Of course I will. All I want is to be where you are, Giselle. You know I would have moved to Paris if you'd asked me to.'

She shook her head. 'You belong where you

are now and so do your children, and though I know you never expected to hear me say it, I feel as if I belong there, too.'

An announcement came over the public address system and she said, 'They're calling my flight, Marc. I have to go, but before I do, there is something I have to ask you.'

'Ask away.'

Placing her overnight bag on the floor beside her, Giselle dropped down on to her knees and said, 'I was going to do this when I got back, but to show you that I mean what I say, will you marry me, Marc?'

Those standing nearby paused in what they were doing and when he cried, 'Yes! Yes! Yes!' a cheer went up.

She'd been everywhere she could think of in the time—Notre Dame, the Louvre, the Champs-Elysées, the Eiffel Tower, her favourite shopping malls. Finally, in a quiet churchyard, Giselle had placed flowers, lots of them, on her mother's grave.

'I love him, *maman*,' she whispered into the silence. 'I love Marc more than words can tell. Be happy for me.'

On the flight back to Manchester there were no regrets inside her. Paris had been just as beautiful as she remembered it, but she'd moved on into a new life in a small Cheshire village and that was where her heart would be forever more.

Marc was waiting for her when the plane landed at Manchester, standing out in the crowd. As their glances met, Giselle knew that she was home where she belonged.

'How was it?' he asked gently as he held her in his arms. 'Did it hurt a lot?'

She shook her head. 'No, not really. I knew all the time I wanted to be here with you.'

'We'll go there for our honeymoon,' he promised.

Smiling up at him, she said, 'Do you think Tom and Alice would approve?'

'What do you mean?' he asked slowly.

'I think you know.'

'You want them to go with us on our honey-moon?'

'Mmm. Why not? We can't leave them behind. They belong with us.'

'You are incredible,' he said.

'No,' she told him. 'It took me a long time to face up to what you were asking of me. That was why I didn't want to sleep with you before I'd made my decision. I knew that once we'd made love I wouldn't be able to think rationally. Not that I ever could when you were around, but I have to warn you that I don't do things by halves and will probably end up more of a country dweller than the villagers themselves.'

'You mean making jam and presiding at the village fête?' he teased.

'I might be able to say a few words at the fête, but I'm not sure about the jam,' she told him laughingly.

As they drove away from the airport Giselle reminded him, 'I told Alice that it would be her turn to be a bridesmaid one day. I hope she won't think that I'm marrying you just to oblige.'

'Talking of weddings, when is it to be?' Marc asked. 'Tomorrow or the day after would suit me fine.'

'What about a Christmas wedding?' she suggested. 'We wouldn't have to take the children out of school for the trip to Paris, for one thing. I could have white velvet and carry a muff covered in flowers instead of a bouquet, and Alice could wear red velvet with a muff.'

'And I could be dressed as Father Christmas,' he teased.

A Christmas wedding it was, as Giselle had described, except that Marc was in a grey morning suit with the traditional top hat and so was Craig, his best man. Philip had wanted the reception to be in a top hotel somewhere, but he had been persuaded to hire the village hall instead so that the whole community could share the special day with their doctor and his new wife.

As Giselle walked down the aisle on her father's arm, with a delighted Alice close behind, there was such a feeling of goodwill all around her that tears were sparkling on her lashes by the time she reached Marc's side.

'What's wrong?' he asked in a low voice. 'Why the tears?'

'Nothing is wrong,' she told him, smiling up at him. 'That is why I'm crying.'

Giselle and Marc might have been able to persuade her father to change his mind about the big hotel for the reception, but they couldn't budge him on one thing.

He'd had Abbeyfields signed over to them and was having a flat built onto it for himself, which reminded her of the day when he'd said, 'You never know, we might all end up living here together. You, me, Marc and the children.'

At that time she hadn't been able to see it happening in a million years but, as Marc said when she told him of her father's generosity, 'I felt when you outbid me that day at the auction that I would somehow still live here one day. I never dared to dream that it would be with you, the woman I love. That makes Abbeyfields all the more the home of my dreams.'

MEDICAL ROMANCE™

 *Large Print*

Titles for the next six months…

October

THE DOCTOR'S UNEXPECTED PROPOSAL
Alison Roberts
THE DOCTOR'S SURPRISE BRIDE — Fiona McArthur
A KNIGHT TO HOLD ON TO Lucy Clark
HER BOSS AND PROTECTOR Joanna Neil
THE SURGEON'S CONVENIENT FIANCÉE Rebecca Lang
THE SURGEON'S MARRIAGE RESCUE Leah Martyn

November

HIS HONOURABLE SURGEON Kate Hardy
PREGNANT WITH HIS CHILD Lilian Darcy
THE CONSULTANT'S ADOPTED SON Jennifer Taylor
HER LONGED-FOR FAMILY Josie Metcalfe
MISSION: MOUNTAIN RESCUE Amy Andrews
THE GOOD FATHER Maggie Kingsley

December

MATERNAL INSTINCT Caroline Anderson
THE DOCTOR'S MARRIAGE WISH Meredith Webber
THE DOCTOR'S PROPOSAL Marion Lennox
THE SURGEON'S PERFECT MATCH — Alison Roberts
THE CONSULTANT'S HOMECOMING Laura Iding
A COUNTRY PRACTICE Abigail Gordon

MILLS & BOON®

Live the emotion

0906 LP 2P P1 Medical

MEDICAL ROMANCE™

 *Large Print*

January

THE MIDWIFE'S SPECIAL DELIVERY   Carol Marinelli
A BABY OF HIS OWN   Jennifer Taylor
A NURSE WORTH WAITING FOR   Gill Sanderson
THE LONDON DOCTOR   Joanna Neil
EMERGENCY IN ALASKA   Dianne Drake
PREGNANT ON ARRIVAL   Fiona Lowe

February

THE SICILIAN DOCTOR'S PROPOSAL Sarah Morgan
THE FIREFIGHTER'S FIANCÉ   Kate Hardy
EMERGENCY BABY   Alison Roberts
IN HIS SPECIAL CARE   Lucy Clark
BRIDE AT BAY HOSPITAL   Meredith Webber
THE FLIGHT DOCTOR'S ENGAGEMENT   Laura Iding

March

CARING FOR HIS CHILD   Amy Andrews
THE SURGEON'S SPECIAL GIFT   Fiona McArthur
A DOCTOR BEYOND COMPARE   Melanie Milburne
RESCUED BY MARRIAGE   Dianne Drake
THE NURSE'S LONGED-FOR FAMILY   Fiona Lowe
HER BABY'S SECRET FATHER   Lynne Marshall

MILLS & BOON®
Live the emotion

0906 LP 2P P2 Medical